56 Sherlock Holmes Stories in 56 Days

Charlotte Anne Walters

Paperback ISBN 9781780922737
ePub ISBN 9781780922744
PDF ISBN 9781780922751

Published in the UK by MX Publishing
335 Princess Park Manor, Royal Drive, London, N11 3GX
www.mxpublishing.com

Cover design by www.staunch.com

Contents

4

56 Stories in 56 Days

Introduction

I still remember handing in my resignation – standing there in the dining room of the pub where I had worked for nine years feeling a mix of sadness and excitement. This was my chance to get my nights back; I already worked full-time during the day and longed for a normal routine - coming home and having all evening to do whatever I wanted. Now, finally I could afford to do it and couldn't wait to spend summer nights walking in the countryside, cycling, having picnics, socialising. But after nine years of dreaming, the reality was quite different. As the weeks stretched by and my nights were filled with nothing more exciting than watching the telly, I decided it was time to take action and begin writing that novel I'd always talked about – you know the one, the novel we would all write if only we had the time. Well, now I had the time.

So Barefoot on Baker Street was born, my debut novel which took seven years to write and was published by MX Publishing in 2011. It is a fictional memoir written in the first-person describing the tumultuous life of workhouse orphan Red and her journey into maturity. During the course of her eventful life she meets Victorian consulting detective Sherlock Holmes and becomes increasingly drawn into his world.

Writing a novel was a wonderful journey of discovery and as the book grew up, so did I. I progressed from being a retail sales temp, single and living above a shop, to a married woman with two step-children, my own home and a job as a senior recruitment manager. My writing grew up too, from rather amateur musings to a full-length novel. A process finally completed with the second edition of Barefoot, re-edited and evolved into the novel I had always hoped I would be able to write.

When I started out writing the novel, my previous experience of freelance journalism did little to prepare me for the rigours of producing such a sustained piece of writing. Fitting it in alongside a busy life was pretty chaotic. But, however hard and long the gestation period, Barefoot on Baker Street was born and emerged into a Sherlock Holmes world very different to how it had been seven years previous.

When I began the process, Sherlock Holmes had rather slipped out of the mainstream, he certainly wasn't cool anymore. This was post-Jeremy Brett and pre-Robert Downey Jr and Benedict Cumberbatch. Writing a novel which involved the character of Holmes was a brave thing to do, and attracted much ridicule from those who became aware of what I was doing. But this was part of the challenge and shaped what the book became, a very accessible story specifically written for both fans and those who have never read a Holmes story in their lives. Now the world seems to have gone Holmes-mad and love for the world's most famous detective is stronger than ever.

I wanted to do something to mark the launch of my novel, something big, Holmesian and challenging. I had used the original canon heavily in my creation of Barefoot and weaved stories and dialogue from it into my own narrative, but it felt like a very long time since I had read the stories purely for pleasure. I had lost touch with the joy and magic of Sir Arthur Conan Doyle's writing.

I wanted to visit the short stories again, immerse myself in the comforting, familiar world of Victorian London with its gas lights and foggy cobbled streets, Holmes and Watson in their fireside chairs awaiting the arrival of a client. It would be comforting, almost like popping round for a cup of tea with old friends.

I fell in love with the Holmesian world from a young age and loved the escapism the stories provided - huddled up in bed after a long day at school with a mug of hot chocolate while the rain lashed the windows, disappearing off to another time and place – guided by the gentle, familiar narration of Doctor Watson.

It was time to re-visit the stories which are at the heart of everything Holmesian, from the blockbuster films to the brilliant BBC Sherlock series and indeed my own novel - and so the 56 Stories project was born. I decided to read and review one Sherlock Holmes short story every day until I had covered all 56.

This sounded easy enough and a great way to re-connect with the canon. But in reality, trying to do this every day on top of my demanding full time job, family commitments, housework and promoting my novel was an absolute challenge. Sitting on the floor of a ridiculously busy commuter train with the laptop on my knee trying to get my blog up on time became a common occurrence, as did the 5am. starts and arguments with my neglected husband who'd heard nothing but Sherlock Holmes from the day we met!

But ultimately, the project was a wonderful experience reminding me of the great skill Conan Doyle possessed in shaping these perfect, concise little tales and the imagination to contrive such a body of work. I reminded myself how literary Doyle's writing could be, his brilliant descriptions of storms and Victorian London sitting neatly alongside the action and drama packed into each tale. And in Sherlock Holmes he has created probably the most famous literary character of all time, one who is known and loved the world over and has inspired countless writers to analyse, re-create and re-invent this most fascinating of men.

At first, my blogs attracted little attention, but as the days passed into weeks, people started to follow the series from all over the world, adding their own comments and urging me to continue. Realising how global the Holmesian fan-base really is was an eye-opener and the support I received was fantastic. Suddenly hundreds of views were turning into thousands and new followers were being added to the site daily. Being able to share my thoughts on an international scale was both exciting and daunting in equal measure. I gave each story a score out of ten and was able to identify what exactly it was I loved so much about Holmes and his world – also the things I wasn't so keen on, such as Irene Adler and stories without Watson.

This book contains all 56 blogs from the series, as well as my reviews of the four long stories. I have also included a break-down of my findings – my top ten and why, bottom ten and why, as well as some interesting details about which blogs attracted the most traffic and comments.

Re-connecting with the skill and detail in the canon was a real education for me, and despite the difficulties I loved every minute of reading and analysing stories which felt as fresh and exciting to me as the first time I had read them as a child. If only I had known back then the journey they would ultimately take me on, a journey which I hope is not yet finished.

For now, I am delighted that a love of writing and a love of Sherlock Holmes came together and inspired me to achieve two published books, a popular blog, connect with a fascinating international fan-base and even get my younger step-son Charlie reading (and loving) the canon. To be able to pass on something from my childhood which I loved so much and know that he is now a Holmes fan too is wonderful – if I can just get him to tidy his bedroom and eat vegetables my life will be complete (until the next project...)

Some thoughts about Undershaw...

Undershaw is the house that Sherlock Holmes creator Sir Arthur Conan Doyle designed, built and made into an elegant family home. Conan Doyle was living at Undershaw when he received his knighthood in 1902 and also where he wrote The Hound of the Baskervilles and The Return of Sherlock Holmes - resurrecting his most famous creation from 'death' at the hands of Professor Moriarty.

Undershaw was an impressive eleven-bedroom house set in beautiful surroundings at Hindhead, Surrey. Apart from the house of Thomas Hardy, Undershaw is the only historic, literary house in England designed by the writer who lived there.

Since 2004, the house and grounds have been owned by a developer who hopes to carve this historic house into three terraced houses, with five more homes to be built on the site. If this happens, Undershaw will be lost forever.

Thanks to the hard work and protestations from the Save Undershaw Campaign, development has been put on hold pending a legal ruling. Sadly, the house has now fallen into disrepair, abandoned to the elements – windows are broken, vandalism has occurred and water has poured in causing much damage.

The fight to save this beautiful, historic building continues and all the royalties from this publication are being donated to the trust.

For more information, please visit the Undershaw Preservation Trust's website – www.saveundershaw.com and join the Undershaw Facebook Page;

www.facebook.com/saveundershaw

I just don't think Irene Adler did anywhere near enough to be *the woman.*

I've always had a problem with this story for that very reason. All she did was have a liaison with the king of Bohemia (well ok, I suppose that's not exactly an everyday sort of occurrence), kept a photo of the two of them together and threatened to expose him when he dumped her for someone of more suitable birth.

Then, when Holmes gains entry into her house disguised as an injured clergyman, she realises that his sudden cries of "Fire!" are false, just as she is about to retrieve the photo and reveal it's hiding place. When Holmes returns the following day to get the photo, she has taken it and fled. Well, surely that's just common sense, not really outwitting him?

And besides, Watson makes it perfectly clear that, 'It was not that (Holmes) felt any emotion akin to love for Irene Adler'.

Watson then goes on to explain that - 'All emotions, and that one particularly, were abhorrent to his cold, precise but admirably balanced mind.' This does indeed suggest that Holmes has never felt love, though certainly doesn't rule out sexual experience, in my opinion. It does also add weight to the argument that Holmes may have had autistic tendencies, or possibly Asperger's syndrome, as I believe a lack of emotion can

12

be a symptom. This is further reinforced by the line – 'While Holmes, who loathed every form of society with his whole Bohemian soul...'

Surely for a woman to capture his heart, she too must be emotionally complex and on the outskirts of society?

For a writer, the opening paragraph of A Scandal gives much inspiration and I certainly have examined such issues in Barefoot. There is also mention in the second paragraph of Holmes' use of cocaine, the drowsiness this gives him and the fierce energy of his own nature. This supports the explanation I present in Barefoot that Holmes' drug use is not to stimulate his mind but rather to quieten it, to subdue the compulsions to observe and the constant rush of mental process which is as much a blessing as a curse to him.

So much from just two paragraphs. To be honest, for me, it all goes a bit downhill from there.

A Scandal in Bohemia scores - 5 out of 10.

On a personal level, re-reading this story brings me some relief on two particular points involving my own novel.

Firstly, I decided to write that Watson lived in Kensington as I remembered this to be so in the original stories but couldn't for the life of me remember in which story I had read it. I looked though my well-thumbed Penguin Complete Sherlock Holmes many times but could not find the Kensington reference. So I was very pleased to read in the Red Headed League that Watson mentions his house in Kensington, meaning that I did get it right after all.

Another point of detail which caused me angst was the furniture issue – what did people sit on in Victorian England? I couldn't keep putting everyone in armchairs and fireside chairs but obviously no-one would sit on the sofa. I therefore took a risk that settee would be an acceptable alternative, even though my husband thought this was still too modern. So when Watson uses the word settee himself on the opening page of The League, I couldn't help but raise a satisfied smile.

At the beginning of the narrative, Holmes rather touchingly refers to Watson as his partner and helper when describing him to Mr Wilson, which is a big improvement on simply biographer. It acknowledges the active role Watson plays in the adventures and the word partner infers an equal status to Holmes which is very interesting. Watson lives up to this description by bravely accompanying Holmes, Jones and the bank director into the cellar of the bank despite Holmes making it clear danger will be involved and an army revolver required.

In the Granada series starring Jeremy Brett as Holmes, the RHL is one of my favourite episodes. It contains a great performance from Richard Wilson (pre Victor Meldrew) as Duncan Ross and Tim McInnerny as John Clay. I seem to recall that the TV dramatisation makes more of the bank director's scepticism at Holmes' suggestion that the gold is to be stolen. It is, of course, always most enjoyable when Holmes proves his doubters wrong.

The story contains much humour and is very clever in its conception. Also, more light is shed upon the workings of Holmes' mind when Watson states – 'The swing of his nature took him from extreme languor to devouring energy,' further suggesting, arguably, a mental instability.

Finally, there is mention of a vegetarian restaurant and I had no idea such a concept existed in Victorian England. There I was fretting about settees being too modern but the folk of late nineteenth century London were actually popping out for hummus and falafel on a regular basis. Great stuff!

The Red Headed League scores 7 out of 10.

There have certainly been times over the many years it has taken me to write my novel when I have worried about the story being a bit too far-fetched at times.

Overall, I don't think it is but, well, I suppose some parts do stretch the imagination somewhat. But clearly I needn't have worried because in A Case of Identity reality is suspended as we are asked to believe this *very* far-fetched tale of a girl and her evil step father.

Poor Miss Mary Sutherland has been duped into believing that someone wishes to marry her and when he disappears she resolves to keep her pledge until he returns. This is what he begged her to do should anything happen to him. The mysterious Mr Hosmer Angel however, is actually her greedy stepfather in disguise. He doesn't want her to leave home and take her £100 a year allowance with her; therefore he concocts this whole saga so that she will resist all suitors for a good few years to come.

Personally, I love this story. It's great fun even though impossible to believe. Despite the stepfather's disguise of beard, side-whiskers, tinted glasses and whispery voice surely his step-daughter would recognise the man she lives with every day? She tells her story to Holmes in a clear, intelligent way so is obviously not stupid. Would she really fall for such a callous trick? Holmes even says to her upon hearing her story – 'You have made your statement very clearly'.

But then, fiction doesn't have to be completely believable does it? Are books not meant to be our escape from the all-to-believable realities of modern life?

I really like the line Holmes says to Watson at the start – 'Life is infinitely stranger than anything which the mind of man could invent.' I think this may have inspired my opening line in Barefoot but actually didn't realise this until reading the story again today - :

'Life in all its complexities is stranger than any fiction and full of so many intricate twists and turns that we sometimes lose track of ourselves, of who we really are.'

Isn't it strange how lines from Holmes stories become so familiar to us that they just become part of our everyday phraseology without us even realising? Or am I just strange like that?

Anyway, other points of interest about this story are that the reader is left in no doubt as to the extent of Holmes' success both in England and internationally. Watson remarks early on how Holmes is a 'Helper to everybody who is absolutely puzzled, through three continents'. Holmes then talks of his work with the King of Bohemia and the reigning family of Holland. He also tells Watson that he has twelve cases on the go – so clearly business is booming!

Quite unusually I think, Holmes is so enraged by the stepfather's behaviour and the lack of official action which can be taken as no actual law has been broken, that he goes to whip him with his hunting crop. This seems to be an uncharacteristically emotive action from such a cold and reasoned man. Holmes does have hidden depths of emotion.

My only problem with the story however, is that Holmes doesn't tell poor Mary the truth and I imagine that she carried on staying true to the non-existent Mr Angel into her old age. How strange that Holmes cared enough to want to whip the man who duped her, but not enough to tell her the truth?

For this reason, I can't give the story any higher than a 6 out of 10, despite enjoying it very much until the last page.

I'm sitting on a train travelling back home from London to the Midlands. My meeting ended early and I arrived back at Euston station in time to walk towards Baker Street, following the route which Red - the protagonist in my novel – would have taken during a key scene.

I had strange Goosebumps at the thought of actually being there, in situ, and imagining how she would have felt running through the streets to reach 221b one stormy early evening.

Anyway, back to the matter in hand. The train journey did give me the perfect opportunity to read the Boscombe Valley Mystery and have a think about what further insights it gives into both Holmes and his partnership with Watson. Partnership seems to be the appropriate word because in this story it is clear how much Holmes needs Watson. He even sends a telegram to Watson's house requesting his company for a few days in the West of England while he investigates this new case.

The telegram arrives as the Watsons are eating breakfast and Mrs Watson urges her husband to go adding – 'You are always so interested in Mr Sherlock Holmes' cases'. Watson replies, 'I should be ungrateful if I were not, seeing what I gained through one of them.'

This confirms that the first Mrs Watson was Mary Morstan from The Sign of Four and I can't believe how blatantly

Guy Ritchie ignored this in his film – more to the point I can't believe how little this seemed to have mattered to Holmes fans as I have seen very little criticism of this error. In the first Sherlock Holmes movie, Watson is engaged to a woman who is clearly not Mary. He has to go and visit her parents (Original Mary's parents were both dead) and she meets Holmes for the first time in a restaurant, not through bringing him the mystery of the Sign of Four. This really mattered to me and coming so early on in the film it did rather spoil my enjoyment (not that Ritchie will mind of course – "Oh I would happily give back all the millions I made if Charlotte Anne Walters would enjoy my film.")

Further evidence of how much Holmes has come to rely on Watson comes later on in the story when he asks him to be a sounding board to help him think through his ideas – 'Look here Watson, just sit down in this chair and let me preach to you for a little. I don't quite know what to do, and I should value your advice. Light a cigar, and let me expound."

What a lovely thing to say, acknowledging not only how much he needs Watson but also that he is at ease enough with him to admit not knowing what to do and to ask his advice.

The case against young James McCarthy looks so solid that as a reader it is almost impossible to see how Holmes will save the day. This makes it all the more satisfying when he does – especially the part where he refers to Lestrade as an 'Imbecile'!

The story does follow a familiar Doyle theme of someone coming to England with ill-gotten gains from the colonies and their past finally catches up with them. I suppose this was just the topic of the age – imperial advances and people becoming more geographically mobile. Am I the only one who sometimes gets the stories muddled up because of this commonality?

Score for the Boscombe Valley Mystery = 7 out of 10

56 stories in 56 days - The Five Orange Pips

The story starts with a very literary description of a storm.

It sees Sir Arthur Conan Doyle reminding us of what a skilful writer he was – not just in terms of narrative but also description, sentence structure and the way he could intersperse short, choppy stories with moments of higher literary form, for example:

'It was in the latter days of September, and the equinoctial gales had set in with exceptional violence. All day the wind had screamed and the rain had beaten against the windows, so that even here in the heart of great, hand-made London we were forced to raise our minds for the instant from the routine of life, and to recognize the presence of those great elemental forces which shriek at mankind through the bars of his civilization, like untamed beasts in a cage. As evening drew in the storm grew louder and louder, the wind cried and sobbed like a child in the chimney.'

Early on in 'the pips' Holmes confirms that Watson is his only friend in response to Watson's question about whether it is a friend who has come to call in such bad weather. I suppose we all knew Holmes to be otherwise friendless but it is surprisingly poignant to hear him say it.

John Openshaw braves the storm and comes to visit Holmes to relate his unusual tale. He sits in the warm, safe, comforting sitting room at 221b and tells Holmes and Watson about the five orange pips delivered to his uncle and father prior to their deaths. As he has now received the ominous pips himself with the sinister KKK written on the envelope he is rightly afraid and motivated to seek help.

But this is where the story rather departs from the usual Holmes formula. Instead of Holmes being the hero and saving the day, he sends the young man away to his death. This does give us an opportunity to see Holmes full of emotion as he feels regret and sadness upon hearing the news – 'It becomes a personal matter with me now', adding, 'that he should come to me for help, and that I should send him away to his death - !'

As with the way he felt compelled by his emotions to threaten Mr Windibank the wicked stepfather in A Case of Identity, here again Holmes displays great emotion and caring towards a client. This is very contrary to our usual image of Holmes as the cold, unemotional thinker who could always control his feelings. He was clearly capable of experiencing deep sentiments, and from a personal point of view this does make plausible incidents which happen in my own novel.

The ending of 'the pips' is also rather unusual as the perpetrators are not caught or even aware that the detective is on their trail. They simply die at sea. That's it. The end. Very disappointing if you ask me.

Yes the story does contain some great examples of Holmes' deduction skills, though not the observing-at-the-scene kind which I personally prefer, but impressive none-the-less. The ending is just too sudden and unsatisfying for me.

A great start, a ponderous middle and unsatisfactory ending. The Five Orange Pips scores 5 out of 10. Sorry Sir Arthur, but I did love your storm.

I have used the story of Mr Neville St. Clair, the faux beggar, extensively in my own novel.

And I can remember exactly the moment at which I had the idea to intertwine the two tales. I was on my honeymoon sitting by the beautiful infinity pool at a lovely hotel on a tranquil Greek Island, writing pad in hand as always.

Without giving away too much about the plot, I was basically playing around with the idea of Professor Moriarty ordering his henchmen to snatch beggars from the city streets. Who would miss a lonely old beggar? Who would even notice he had gone? But then the idea struck me - what if the person wasn't really a beggar but actually in disguise? What if he did have a concerned family who would contact Holmes for help – drawing him into the crime which would ultimately put him onto a collision course with my protagonist? Perfect.

I reached into my beach-bag for the ever present Penguin Complete Sherlock Holmes and re-read The Man with The Twisted Lip then celebrated my brainwave with a lovely Greek salad while looking out to sea.

Upon re-reading the story today it's hard to put my own story aside and just comment on the original. It's just that it proved to be so pivotal in my own tale and such a perfect example of what I wanted to do with Barefoot – intertwine the original stories with my own in a sensitive and imaginative way

25

without simply trying to re-create Doyle's style but instead using this as inspiration to create something which both new and existing Holmes fans would love.

It seems like such a long time ago (I've been married four years now) when I had that moment of inspiration beside the infinity pool (incidentally, it was the best hotel pool I've ever had the pleasure to lie next to). I had no idea how much hard work lay ahead to actually finish my novel but was full of hope and optimism that I could change my life and achieve my dream of becoming a bestselling author.

Anyway, apologies for the serious digression and back to the story.

What is going on between Sherlock Holmes and Mrs Neville St. Clair? There is something very odd about this one.

When Watson goes to rescue his patient from the opium den and finds Holmes inside, they leave together and Holmes asks Watson to accompany him as he investigates his latest case, casually pointing out that his room - '...at the Cedars is a double-bedded one'. 'The Cedars?' asks Watson, perplexed. 'Yes; that is Mr St Clair's house. I am staying there while I conduct the inquiry'.

This presents various points of interest from the casual way he refers to her home, to the issue of why he needs to be there in the first place.

The Cedars is in Lee, Kent, and perfectly commutable from London. Mrs St Claire isn't in any danger, the house is not the scene of the crime, the man disappeared in the city not at home, so why on earth is Holmes staying there in a double bedded room – and why does Mrs St Clair answer the door to him wearing a 'Mousseline-de-soie with a touch of fluffy pink chiffon at her neck and wrists'? Good God it's like 'Carry On Detecting'.

Other points of interest are the fact that Holmes is more than happy to share his room with Watson (though not the bed) and this shows the extent to which he feels comfortable with him. This is also the story in which he talks of Watson's 'Grand gift of silence,' which makes him 'quite invaluable as a companion'. The Man with the Twisted Lip clearly, and rather touchingly, demonstrates the depth of their friendship.

Fluffy pink chiffon aside, the most unusual thing about this tale is the fact that Dr John H Watson suddenly becomes James - according to his wife. A mystery all of its own, or just a Conan Doyle mistake?

I really enjoyed re-reading this story – as much for the comedic value and personal memories as anything – and will happily score it an hilarious 8 out of 10.

56 stories in 56 days - The Adventure of the Blue Carbuncle

This is another of the short stories which features in my own novel. And gosh was it hard work to adapt it to what I wanted.

I spent many a stressful hour going over every detail of the original and trying to keep things largely the same but add my own protagonist into the plot.

In the story, the upper attendant at the Cosmopolitan Hotel steals a precious stone called the blue carbuncle from the countess of Morcar who is staying there. He causes a little damage in the room and sends for a plumber – John Horner – who has a previous conviction for robbery, and then blames him for the theft. Throw in the complication of how he then escapes with the stone and hides it by forcing a Christmas goose to swallow it and you have a very jolly, neat, tale.

All I had to do was make my central character, Red, the one who steals the stone while trying to keep everything else the same. Sounds simple? Well, it took days. But I have to say that the end result is one of my favourite parts of the novel and has kept some of the humour of the original too. And boy, did the original make me laugh at times.

The Blue Carbuncle contains what I believe to be one of the funnies lines in all the Holmes stories, not least because it wasn't intentional. When Holmes finally apprehends Ryder, he brings him back to 221b and must surely be dying to hear his story but takes an unexpected pause – 'You look cold, Mr

Ryder. Pray take the basket chair. I will just put on my slippers before we settle this little matter of yours.' Maybe it's just my singular sense of humour but I read that and laughed so hard tears rolled down my cheeks. "I'll just go and put my slippers on," is like something my Nan would have said, not the world's greatest consulting detective.

Holmes concludes the adventure by saying to Watson – "If you have the goodness to touch the bell, Doctor, we will begin another investigation, in which also a bird will be the chief feature." Doyle put much humour into his writing and I do think this is often, sadly, overlooked.

The Blue Carbuncle also contains a perfect example of the science of deduction at its best. Holmes examines an old hat and deduces from it that the wearer is of high intelligence, was once rather well-to-do but has since fallen on hard times, his wife no longer loves him and he has gas laid on in his house. It's simply brilliant and at first the reader is as baffled as Watson but once the reasoning is explained it is so simple. Such as with the pocket Watch analysis in the Sign of Four, so much is gained from so little. It is this 'science' which makes Holmes so different to other fictional detectives and makes him such a fascinating character.

Holmes' social isolation is further reinforced in this story. Except for Watson's visit he is alone at Christmas. Peterson the commissionaire does visit on Christmas Day but only because he needs Holmes' help.

The story is another example of how Holmes exercises his own unique sense of justice. He listens to Ryder's story (once he has put his slippers on) and decides to let him go. To have that level of assurance in your own judgement shows a high level of self-confidence. It also demonstrates just how separately Holmes operates from the official police. This combines to give the overall impression of someone independent, a touch eccentric and very much their own man. These are the very attributes that have always drawn me to Holmes as a character.

A great little story with brilliant deduction and humour – 8 out of 10.

This is a funny one really because though I enjoyed re-reading the story, I can't really think of much to say about it.

I suppose there is lots to say about the stories I love and plenty to get off my chest about those I don't like, but this one comes somewhere in the middle. Plus, it's wages day today at work and I've been staring at a spread-sheet all day so my brain feels too stuck in the 21st century to really loose itself in the 19th.

That's one of the things that made writing my Holmes novel difficult, switching between two eras when my job firmly places me in the modern world of prestige-cosmetics recruitment, a million miles from Victorian London. Some weekends I'd be sitting there writing about foggy cobbled streets with hansom cabs rattling along, then I'd get a phone call about epic staffing disasters on a make-up counter in a prestige department store and be pulled abruptly back into the 21st century. Sometimes it was hard to make my way back.

So what can I say about the Speckled Band? It certainly draws you in and all seems very plausible at the time, but when you think about it afterwards, some things do seem unrealistic.

Holmes was very lucky not to have been bitten by the snake (the speckled band) as he thrashed it with his stick and I doubt you can train a snake with a whistle and the promise of a saucer of milk. Also, could someone really have kept a baboon and a cheetah strolling around their gardens?

But, as I say, this doesn't distract from the enjoyment as you read the story. It is one of the only short stories where I have found myself working things out ahead of Watson but it still kept me gripped all the way home on the train. I nearly missed my stop because I was so lost in the tale of poor Miss Stoner and her evil step-father.

Conan Doyle clearly has little regard for step-fathers as they are generally portrayed as eager to get their hands on their charge's money by any means. In this case, by sending a poisonous snake into Miss Stoner's room at night then calling it back with the aforementioned whistle and milk.

Once again Holmes seems to genuinely care about his client and it is interesting to read the stories back like this and see the kindness and sensitivity Holmes was capable of.

He is also quite protective of Watson in this story, pointing out the danger they will face and thanking him for agreeing to spend the night with him in the room where the first snake-victim met their end. When they cross the grounds to the house and encounter the baboon, Holmes grabs Watson's wrist to stop him walking on further. He is also careful to position Watson in a chair away from the bed whilst Holmes himself sits on the bed next to the rope which the snake will descend.

Enjoyable and diverting, but a little unrealistic – 6 out of 10.

56 Stories in 56 Days - The Adventure of the Engineer's Thumb

This is a curious story, gripping but very different to the usual formula.

On the one hand, as a stand-alone short story about a hydraulic engineer who inadvertently goes off to fix a press used in coin forging and gets him thumb cut off by a cruel German baddie, it's a really absorbing little story. The part where the poor young man is trapped inside the press with it coming down on top of him is as exciting as an action sequence from Indiana Jones. But on the other hand, as a Holmes adventure, it gives little opportunity to see the detection and observation that makes up the usual formula we know and love.

There is, of course, Holmes' observation that the horse which pulled the carriage from the station to the mystery forging house was 'Fresh and glossy' and therefore hadn't travelled far to reach it.

This explained much about the location of the forging press but was irrelevant really as the column of smoke billowing from its ruins gave away its location anyway. Holmes was also the one who linked the incident to a previous disappearance of a hydraulic engineer but this too didn't lead to any particular resolution, except for suggesting that the German had form in his murdering ways.

But that's it really; Holmes has very little impact beyond these two points. But does that matter when the story is as neat and concise as this one? And what of the ending? The villains escape but the crushing of the engineer's oil lamp in the press has caused the whole forging operation to be swallowed by flames. I suppose this is a closure of sorts but I was left wanting more – more deduction and more comeuppance.

Fast and gripping, but more 'short story' rather than 'Sherlock Holmes short story' – 7 out of 10.

A joyous story of Holmes at his best and featuring strong female characters.

Miss Hatty Doran, the feisty American tomboy is a great character together with her loyal maid Alice; and so too is Flora Millar, the former danseuse at the Allegro who is clearly the woman for whom Lord St Simon feels the most genuine affection.

The story starts off with Watson lounging around on a rainy autumn day feeling a bit sorry for himself and nursing his war-wound – the Jezail bullet stuck in a limb – though the exact location of it is not specified. As Holmes admirers know, there is confusion about this as it is described as being in both the shoulder and the leg in two different stories. As I refer to it in my own novel, it was strange to be reminded of Watson's injury in the original text as the scene in which the wound is mentioned in Barefoot is so pivotal and brings about a shocking epiphany in my main character.

But back to Lord St Simon and his vanishing bride. Gosh he is an awful snob isn't he? And isn't it fun watching Holmes bring him down a rung or two; -

St Simon – 'I understand that you have already managed several delicate cases of this sort, sir, though I presume that they were hardly from the same class of society.'

Holmes – 'No, I am descending.'

St Simon – 'I beg pardon?'

Holmes – 'My last client of the sort was a king.'

I do love the way that Holmes is unaffected by personages of class and is generally un-materialistic and unpretentious. While most of the middle classes at that time, which I guess is what Holmes was, were trying so desperately to climb higher, all he wanted was interest and stimulation regardless of who brought it to him.

Watching Lestrade blundering around coming to all the wrong conclusions and missing the most significant of details is always fun and this story is a prime example of it. He hits upon the simplest explanation for the lady's disappearance and for a time we almost go along with it, but keen readers know from Holmes' overly congratulatory response heavy with sarcasm, that the hapless official had got it wrong yet again. He baits Holmes and we excitedly wait for Holmes to have his moment.

I love this story, a feel-good tale of the ordinary man getting the girl and true love winning through. The official and the toff are put in their place by a gutsy American woman and a clever, eccentric amateur. A well-deserved 8 out of 10.

56 Stories in 56 Days – The Adventure of the Beryl Coronet

Holmes is full of energy in this one, analysing footprints at great length, charging around in disguise and even holding a gun to the head of a villain – it's like a film by Guy Ritchie. The story of private banker Alexander Holder loaning money to a royal personage and keeping the priceless beryl coronet as security, takes on a dramatic turn when parts of the jewel go missing. He catches his son with the remainder in his hand beside the bureau from which it had been taken.

As is often the case, all against the wayward young man looks hopeless and only Holmes is confident of his innocence. We then follow Holmes as he unravels the mystery and finds the missing stones in his own unique way. This involves lots of detailed footprint analysis, disguising himself as a common loafer and having a sprightly exchange with the real villain who is a typical cad – a sort of Dorian Grey type who has made the banker's niece fall so in love with him that she would betray her own family for him.

I have always enjoyed the escapism element to the Holmes stories, the way they draw you into another time and it's not just the narrative which captures the reader, but also the settings, the epoch itself. At the start of this story Watson paints such a lovely scene that for a moment you are right there with him in the sitting room at 221b with Sherlock Holmes, a fire burning in the grate, cosy and warm as snow lays on the ground outside and a bitter wintery air pervades over Victorian London.

The story is also noteworthy for containing the famous line spoken by Holmes – 'When you have excluded the impossible, whatever remains, however improbable, must be the truth.'

Also rather noteworthy, but for a less positive reason, is the incestuous love the son has for his cousin. This is made even more-so by the fact that his father really wanted them to marry, even though she was like a daughter to him and called him Dad. Was marriage between first cousins acceptable then in Victorian times? I thought they were more prudish than modern society and such a thing would have been unthinkable but clearly I am wrong.

I have to say that I did feel a bit sorry for poor Mary at the end, running away with a ruthless player and losing her family, certain to face much heartache. Yes, I know she probably deserved it after stealing the coronet and handing it to him but haven't we all done foolish things for love at least once in our lives?

Good deduction, love, incest and family troubles – what more can you want in a story? – 7 out of 10.

This story reveals much about the difficult nature of Holmes' personality.

The Copper Beeches starts with Holmes being very critical of Watson's accounts of his work. And though Watson answers in such a way as to demonstrate his hurt at such comments, Holmes ignores this and continues regardless. Watson admits to being repelled by, 'The egotism which I had more than once observed to be a strong factor in my friend's singular character'.

It's more than egotism to me, it's as if Holmes just doesn't notice that he has caused offence, can't read the signs or understand the general pragmatics of conversation which involve listening to the other person and responding appropriately. Watson even states that Holmes responds to his thoughts and not his words. During this interchange, Holmes does however say one of my favourite Holmesian quotes – 'Crime is common. Logic is rare.'

I do think this interchange between them adds weight to the argument that Holmes was mildly autistic. There is another odd hint in this story. The child which Miss Hunter is asked to care for could arguably be seen as having signs of autism – 'He is small for his age, with a head which is quite disproportionately large. His whole life appears to be spent in alternation between savage fits of passion and gloomy intervals of sulking.' Is this a subtle clue from Sir Arthur or am I over-analysing?

But then we come to another scene which fits the argument so well. As Holmes and Watson sit on their train travelling through the beautiful English countryside on an idyllic spring day, Watson comments on the beauty of their surroundings prompting Holmes to give a very revealing insight into the workings of his mind – 'It is one of the curses of a mind with a turn like mine that I must look at everything with reference to my own special subject. You look at these scattered houses, and you are impressed by their beauty. I look at them, and the only thought which comes to me is a feeling of their isolation and of the impunity with which crime may be committed there'. Too much evidence to be ignored in my opinion.

Yet again we are treated to a very literary description of the weather at the beginning of the narrative – 'A thick fog rolled down between the lines of dun-coloured houses, and the opposing windows loomed like dark, shapeless blurs through the heavy yellow wreaths.' Sometimes it feels as if Doyle was torn between being a writer of action, dramatic fast-paced tales, or a wordy descriptive writer of higher aspirations.

But now to Miss Violet Hunter and her strange little problem. She comes to see Holmes to take his advice on whether or not she should accept a well-paid position of governess with an eccentric rural family. Holmes is unusually impressed by her manner – 'I could see that Holmes was favourably impressed by the manner and speech of his new client'.

Later on in the story when Holmes sets Miss Hunter a task, he compliments her further by saying – 'I should not ask it of you if I did not think you a quite exceptional woman'. Wow, high praise indeed.

Watson expresses his disappointment towards the end of the story that Holmes doesn't continue with his interest in Miss Hunter once the case is resolved. Clearly he was keen for his friend to show his human side and perhaps form a romantic union. Is the fact that he does not, further proof of autistic tendencies? Or did he just not really fancy her all that much?

As to the plot – well I think it is very far-fetched and I can't really warm to it. Very interesting for what it reveals (or rather hints) about Holmes but that's it for me really. 6 out of 10.

Today is my husband's birthday and therefore it is quite a coincidence that I should be writing about Silver Blaze, as it is his favourite Sherlock Holmes story.

Husband used to be a racing journalist and remains a very knowledgeable admirer of the sport. I suppose it is quite natural therefore, that Silver Blaze should be his favourite. As today is his birthday, my little blogging challenge is causing a degree of friction between us. He wanted to go out for the day, have Sunday lunch in a lovely country pub and spend the afternoon walking together before celebrating with a few friends tonight – but what about the blog? My suggestion that we stayed in tonight so that I could re-read Silver Blaze and write my blog was met with – "It's like you're having an affair with Sherlock Holmes, he certainly gets more of your attention than I do."

I must admit that trying to cope with my full time job at our busiest time of year, helping to look after my mother who has dementia and write this daily blog is quite a challenge. Yes, husband is being neglected.

So as I will be out tonight, here's a quick round-up of my thoughts on Blaze, which is easy really because I absolutely love the story too and re-reading it was a pleasure.

Followers of my blogs will know that Blaze was my favourite Granada episode because they captured the humour and adventure aspect of the original so perfectly, and Jeremy Brett was on top form.

But the actual story has much to shout about too from the playful way Holmes toys with a sceptical colonel Ross to the way he deduces the truth about what really happened to the thoroughbred out on the moor.

Everything is brilliant; the way Holmes knows that the stable boy was poisoned because the curry would have been strong enough to disguise it, the discovery of the groom's double-life, the significance of the lame sheep and, of course, the immortal line about the curious incident of the dog in the night-time. What's not to love in this clever, inventive tale? 9 out of 10.

Oh what a lovely ending, how very touching.

I confess that I had forgotten what happened in this story and hadn't re-read it for years. So the ending came as quite a surprise and was probably a little unconventional at the time.

Effie Munro is a woman with a secret and her husband goes to see Holmes in the hope that he can discover it. This is one of those rare occasions when Holmes gets things completely wrong and the truth is uncovered without his help. The only glimpse of deduction we get is when Holmes analyses Grant Munro's pipe which he leaves behind at 221b. Strangely, Mrs Munro refers to her husband as Jack, not Grant. Is Sir Arthur getting confused over names again or was Grant Munro a surname?

We know from the husband's testimony that his wife had been married before in America but her husband and child had died in a fire. She came to England with a good income and married Grant/Jack. They had been happily married for three years and suddenly she asked for a large sum of money which he happily gave but was suspicious as she wouldn't reveal what she wanted it for. Then mysterious neighbours moved into a nearby cottage and he saw a pale, rigid face at the window. His wife started to make secretive visits to the cottage and wouldn't reveal why.

Holmes concludes that the American husband must have tracked her down and is now blackmailing her. Perhaps she ran away from him for being a cruel man rather than him dying in a fire?

But this theory is wrong and the truth came as quite a surprise. Her first husband was black and the child black also.

She leaves the little girl in America because of her fragile health and travels to England alone. Upon meeting her new husband she is afraid to tell him the truth in case he leaves her and she is forced to try and forget the child.

I remarked to husband that this seemed very unrealistic but he reminded me of the times in which it was set and the strength of feeling still prevalent about people of a different colour.

This makes the ending even more lovely, as the husband upon discovery of the child and his wife's secret, – 'Lifted the child, kissed her, and then, still carrying her, he held his other hand out to his wife and turned towards the door; "I am not a very good man Effie, but I think that I am a better one than you have given me credit for being." I had a lump in my throat at that point. The fact that she describes her former husband in glowing terms is also rather lovely.

I'm not a Doyleian expert and don't know what his attitudes towards race were but from this story I'm guessing he was rather ahead of his time.

Other points of interest are that Watson mentions Holmes' use of cocaine – 'As a protest against the monotony of existence when cases were scanty and the papers uninteresting'.

I have argued in my novel that Watson got this wrong and Holmes actually used cocaine to relax and quieten his mind rather than stimulate it. If he did not have work to channel his over-active mind into, he would use drugs to calm it, as a control mechanism not a stimulant. Slightly controversial theory but I think it has legs all the same.

A very heart-warming story without much Holmes but with some forward-thinking attitudes which are very refreshing - 8 out of 10.

I do have a personal reason for enjoying this story. The action mainly takes place in Birmingham, Corporation Street to be precise. I have worked in Birmingham for more than ten years, many of which were in a large department store on Corporation Street. I now have an office not far from there and pass both Corporation Street and New Street (which is also mentioned) most days. Holmes fans from outside of London do envy those in the capital who have such significant locations right on their doorstep and I had quite forgotten that I had two of my own which I pass regularly. I will never look at them quite the same again and shall exhibit a knowing smile on my way to work tomorrow morning.

The story begins with Holmes visiting Watson at his home. We have further proof that the first Mrs Watson was indeed Mary from the Sign of Four when Holmes enquires, rather thoughtfully, – 'I trust that Mrs Watson has entirely recovered from all the little excitements connected with our adventure of The Sign of Four'. I must make the point again that I was very disappointed that Guy Ritchie disregarded this fact in his film and am so surprised that other Sherlockians didn't seem to mind.

Holmes asks Watson to accompany him straight away to Birmingham with his client, Mr Hall Pycroft, and Watson readily agrees to drop everything and go. This involves asking his neighbour, who is also a doctor, to take over his patients while he is gone.

Poor Watson, he really isn't a very good businessman is he? Sending your clients to your competitor while you go off to have an adventure with your friend isn't really a sensible idea now is it? Surely his patients would be quite disgruntled by this new arrangement? And if they get treated well by the other doctor, they might not return.

In my novel, I have used Watson's lack of business acumen to great effect and looked at how the doctor's business and finances were affected by Holmes, particularly by their trip to Switzerland in The Final Problem.

Mr Hall Pycroft gained a good job at a stockbrokers in London but gets enticed away by a better offer in Birmingham – which ultimately turns out to be a ruse so that an imposter (his new boss's brother) can take up the original position and stage a robbery. Confused, I was too to be honest.

Upon hearing that the robbery had been foiled by a very conscientious policeman who notices someone coming out of the stockbrokers after the time they normally shut, the brother tries to kill himself. What a different age it was, when it was unusual to see an employee leaving a building after normal office hours and how quaint that the bobby-on-the-beat would know what time the business shut and follow up his hunch.

Now we work all hours; I regularly leave my office building after it has shut or long before it opens and rarely ever see a policeman/woman, let alone get stopped by one.

The story is fine, nothing remarkable about it really except the local connection and it is another one where Holmes doesn't really do anything to bring about the conclusion.

6 out of 10.

This story is of importance because it documents Holmes' first case, of sorts.

In The Gloria Scott we hear about how a young Holmes went to stay with a college friend, his only friend at the time, and made some astute observations to his father causing the old man to faint.

There then comes a strange old drunkard to visit, a rude man of nautical persuasion who obviously knows a secret which the father wishes to hide. He blackmails him into offering employment.

Interestingly, it is the father who suggests to Holmes a career as a detective and sets him on the path which we all know so well. It is also interesting that even in his early life, Holmes was antisocial. Victor Trevor was, by his own admission, Holmes' only friend at college and we are treated to an interesting insight into Holmes' early personality – 'I was never a very sociable fellow, Watson, always rather fond of moping in my rooms and working out my own little methods of thought, so that I never mixed much with the men of my year'.

Victor was also friendless; Holmes is clearly drawn to loners and those on the outside of society. Watson too was friendless when they first met having just arrived in the capital fresh from a military campaign. This is why, in my own novel, when looking at the issue of what kind of woman could capture

Holmes' heart, I concluded that he would only feel drawn to someone who was also on the outside of normal society, an eccentric outcast. There has always been something a bit too normal about Irene Adler for me.

There is another Birmingham reference in this story but only a passing mention and not a very positive one. Old Mr Trevor's daughter had visited the city, caught diphtheria and died. Not one to shout about for us Brummies.

It turns out that Mr Trevor senior was once a convict on board a ship bound for Australia and, along with fellow prisoners, took control of the vessel and escaped. The old sailor who turns up at the house whilst Holmes is staying there was one of the crew and threatens to reveal his secret.

Holmes doesn't actually do anything to help matters as Mr Trevor dies of a weak heart and leaves his son a letter revealing all. Not really a first case then, more of a being-in-the-right-place-at-the-right-time sort of thing.

I do always feel a little short changed when Holmes doesn't save the day and did find this story a bit too far-fetched. I also missed having Watson's usual involvement.

Just 5 out of 10 I'm afraid. Husband has just looked over my shoulder and feels this mark was a bit harsh, but that's because he had confused the story with the naval treaty so not a valid opinion really. Sorry Tim. My blog, my marks – especially if you can't even get the stories right!

The story begins with a light-hearted description of Watson's despair at Holmes' untidiness, and who could blame him?

The letters fixed to the mantelpiece with a dagger, the tobacco in the Persian slipper, the VR shot into the wall; such untidiness reminds me of my old housemate who used to leave a bottle of milk out on the side for weeks, 'just to see what happens'.

Watson finally asks Holmes to tidy up his mass of paperwork and Holmes brings out a tin box full of old cases to sort through. He pulls out various items originating from what is, in my opinion, his first real case. Though the Gloria Scott is generally regarded as the first, Holmes does not use his skills to solve it as the truth comes out without his intervention, but the conclusion of the Musgrave Ritual is entirely down to Holmes' brilliant deductions. It also follows the pattern more closely in terms of a client coming to visit and asking for help because the official police are baffled.

Retelling the case to Watson gives Holmes the perfect excuse to get out of the tidying up, just like when my old housemate said he couldn't possibly tidy the kitchen because to him, 'Hygiene is a tall woman from Bolton'. High Jean? I know, it took me a while too…

Reginald Musgrave had been at the same college as Holmes and they had 'A slight acquaintance'. Like Victor

Trevor, Musgrave was also a bit of a loner and quite unpopular. Clearly Holmes gravitated to such people and here again it leads to an adventure.

Holmes has newly arrived in London (pre Watson days) and takes rooms in Montague Street then sets about trying to make a name for himself in his chosen profession. Musgrave brings him a great opportunity to do so as no-one else has been able to solve the mystery of his missing butler and maid.

I love the description of Musgrave's wonderful old country pile, I'm right there with them stomping around between the oak and Elm in my tweeds. How lovely it must have been to have belonged to the gentry, inherit a sprawling country estate and spend your days managing it – no nine-to-five job, no daily commute to work, instead just passing time surrounded by the wonders of rural England.

Reading this story on my train at 7.40am travelling into Birmingham to begin a long day's work at my desk, it makes me really sad that I can't spend all my days in the countryside which I love so much. I have long aspired to own an old country house and pootle around my estate all day ridding my horses and walking my dogs (I do live in a barn conversion in a lovely rural town so don't feel too sorry for me) and felt a million miles from that dream as the train pulled into New Street station this morning. Perhaps if my novel becomes a best-seller, then a film etc… Ah, the power of dreams.

Anyway, back to poor Reginald Musgrave (isn't that just the best name of any of the clients?) and his vanishing household.

Holmes cleverly works out that the strange ritual which each young man is required to say before inheriting the estate is actually the key to the whole mystery as it is basically the instructions in a treasure hunt leading to none other than a crown once owned by Charles the Second. The clever butler had worked this out and was trying to steal it with the help of the maid but got trapped in the cellar where the treasure was hidden and died. The maid fled, possibly because she was the one who trapped him there.

This is all fine except the fact that none of the many generations of Musgraves who had recited the ritual had ever figured out the truth behind it. The butler managed it, as did Holmes, with relative ease, so why not the people it affected most?

This last point aside, this is a fantastic story with Holmes at his energetic best. The logic and workings out are brilliant, but we still have Watson to remind us of his short-comings and eccentricities. Very enjoyable indeed – 9 out of 10. And husband agrees this time.

56 Stories in 56 Days - The Reigate Puzzle

Does anyone know why none of the stories in the Memoirs are called 'The Adventure Of' as so many are in the other compilations?

This point has just occurred to me as I typed up the title and I'm sure there is a Holmesian scholar out there who knows the answer.

It's off to the countryside again for another adventure amongst lovely old houses and country squires.

Watson tells us that Holmes has been made ill by his exertions during a difficult case. He is laid up in a hotel room in Lyon and as soon as Watson hears of this, he sets off at once and is at his friend's bedside within twenty-four hours. How did he get there so fast? In this day and age we would just jump on a plane but surely you couldn't get all the way from London to Lyon in twenty-four hours with only a moment's notice all those years ago?

Upon returning to London together, Watson takes Holmes off to stay with an old friend at his country house. Watson tells us that poor Holmes has been working fifteen hours a day, sometimes for five days straight in order to solve an international case and this brought about his sudden illness.

Well, not wishing to belittle Holmes' efforts but I worked nights for many years on top of a full-time day job doing those sorts of hours and I didn't fall ill nor get rushed off for a stay in a lovely old country house to recuperate. Do I sound bitter? Surely not…

Watson describes Holmes as being in the - 'Blackest depression,' reminding us again of Holmes' propensity for extreme mood swings and mental instability.

Once in the countryside, Reigate in Surrey, Holmes gets drawn into the mystery of a spate of local burglaries, one of which ended in the death of a coachman. A fragment of a note is left in the dead man's hand and Holmes uses this to unravel the whole mystery and uncover that it was actually the two gentlemen (father and son) for whom the coachman worked. They had broken in to their neighbour's house to steal an important document relating to land rights and conspired to murder the coachman who knew of this and was blackmailing them.

There's something about this one that just doesn't add up for me. Can't explain it really but everything from Holmes' analysis of the note to the fact that the rest of it is still in the dressing gown pocket of the murderer just seems unrealistic. Surely if you had bothered to snatch the note, you would destroy it straight away? You would also notice some was left behind – wouldn't you? And then there's the way the murdering pair turn on Holmes while Watson, the Colonel and police sergeant are in the room next door – I can understand wanting to silence him but let's face it, they were never going to get away with that one.

How could they explain it anyway? He slipped and strangled himself?

This is an interesting little story that reminds us of the genuine affection and concern Watson had for Holmes but left more questions than answers for me. 6 out of 10.

56 Stories in 56 Days – The Crooked Man

This is another story in which Watson drops everything to go to assist his friend.

Holmes turns up at Watson's house late one summer's evening and asks to stay. He expresses his desire that Watson travel with him to Aldershot the following day to assist in the case he is working on. Watson enthusiastically agrees to both requests, despite it being clear from Holmes' deduction that the doctor has a heavy workload at that time. Once again he passes off his poor patients onto a fellow doctor so that he can go on the adventure. And what a strange little adventure it proves to be.

I have recently re-read my novel (how on earth I found the time with things being so manic at work and all this blogging is impossible to say) and I was concerned about a latter few chapters which are arguably rather 'romantic' in theme. Though none-Holmes readers will probably think nothing of this, I have been concerned that the more traditional Holmes fan-base will not take to it and prefer instead action, crime etc. But then, having just read the Crooked Man, it has occurred to me that most of the original Holmes stories involve love in one form or another.

Here again we have a story about a woman who believes the person she really loves to be dead so marries another, only to discover years later that he is alive and her husband had a hand in her lover's fate. A bit like the American, Hatty Doran, in the

Noble Bachelor, who thought her first lover had died and is shocked to see him in the front pew on her wedding day to Lord St Simon.

Clearly love played a massive part in the short stories which we all know and love so well. As love is the foundation of our lives in one form or another, I really shouldn't worry about the fact that it plays its part in the life of the character I have created in my novel. And besides, it's only a few chapters out of twenty-two which are fast-paced and full of action so surely that will be ok? Won't it?

Back to the crooked man who suddenly sees the woman he loved and wanted to marry in his youth in India, before another suitor set him up and led him into a rebel ambush. After revealing the truth to her out in the street, he follows her home and walks in on her arguing with her husband about the matter.

Upon seeing the man he thought was long dead, the husband suffers a seizure and dies instantly, banging his head on the fender on the way down.

The man flees and everything points to murder by the wife, but Holmes cleverly unravels the truth. However, he does not reveal all to the police and exercises his own judgement on the matter. It becomes clear to the police anyway that the man died of natural causes.

The story is another example of Holmes solving a problem for its own sake, not for glory, money or reputation. And poor Watson's patients pay the price yet again. 8 out of 10.

Watson sits in the rooms at 221b on a rainy day in October longing to go on a holiday which he can't afford. I'm not surprised he's broke considering the way he abandons his patients to chase off after Holmes at every opportunity.

Holmes shocks Watson at the start by seeming to read his mind, and it is rather brilliant that by just observing where his friend looks in the room, how he raises a hand to his old war wound, and the movement of his eyebrows, Holmes knows what he is thinking. Not only is this a fantastic demonstration of the method which Holmes uses to reach his conclusions and the unusual way he sees the world, but also how very well he knows his only friend. He also seems to sense that Watson is in a 'Brown study' and suggests they go for an evening walk together which lifts Watson from his unhappiness. Sherlock Holmes can actually be rather sweet when he wants to be.

Upon returning from their evening walk, the two friends find a visitor waiting for them by the name of Dr Percy Trevelyan. I do sympathise with this young man's story. He is a very skilled man who excelled at university but is not of wealthy birth and therefore cannot jump the queue to success and buy all the trappings he needs to become a successful doctor - impressive premises, horse and carriage etc. So instead he resolves to start small and perhaps in ten years have earned enough to set up as a specialist in his chosen field.

I have known many young people in this position who have turned up at my office looking for retail work because they needed to earn some money before continuing with studies or doing unpaid work experience in the profession they aspire to. Other young people seem to have the resources to do what they want without these diversions and this does often seem unfair. Fortunately, in my role as manager of a temp agency I am able to help a little but the work isn't fantastically paid and I have known many a gifted young person who has had to give up their dreams.

So I really like Dr Trevelyan and understand the sense of elation he must have felt when a wealthy patron, Mr Blessington, comes forward to offer assistance and make all his dreams come true. That's what I need, someone to step forward out of the shadows to make my dreams of being a full time writer come true.

Hurrah then for Mr Blessington but what a shame he lands up dead, and am I the only person left wondering what will become of the poor young doctor now that his funding has been cut off?

Mr Blessington was clearly afraid for his life but wouldn't tell Holmes the truth about his past on his first visit, prompting Holmes to simply walk away from the case. I wonder if perhaps, Holmes should have felt some guilt therefore when the man was murdered that very night? Perhaps if he had tried a bit harder to extract the truth a tragedy could have been avoided?

But then as he was such a scoundrel in his past anyway, perhaps Holmes felt as if justice had been done.

Everything points to suicide but Holmes' brilliant deduction at the scene – very CSI – particularly involving the cigar ash, leads to a very conclusive verdict of murder and the truth about Blessington's past being comprehensively revealed.

I really enjoyed returning to this story and will happily give it 8 out of 10.

56 Stories in 56 Days - The Greek Interpreter

This story has one main point of interest - the formidable Mycroft Holmes.

This is the first story in which we meet the eccentric, but brilliant, Mycroft and this singular character does much to advance the argument that Holmes might have been autistic. The fact that his brother possesses the same traits of observation, incredible memory and antisocial nature does suggest a genetic link behind these characteristics.

Let's look at the facts, Mycroft is so antisocial that he becomes a founder member of a gentleman's club where members are forbidden from talking to each other, he carves out a unique professional position for himself just as his brother has done, and is also without a wife or children. He has an incredible capacity for numbers and accountancy suggesting even Savantism, rather than simply autism.

Watson reminds us in the first paragraph about Holmes' unemotional character, his disinclination to form friendships, his aversion to women. By reminding us of this, he is prompting us to see the similarities between the brothers and the genetic predisposition they share. The story itself is quite absorbing but somehow eclipsed by the revelation of an elder brother and what this tells us about Holmes himself.

Mycroft features heavily in my novel and is another example of how much the Granada series shaped my image of

63

certain characters. Whenever I think of Mycroft I always picture Charles Grey and that is basically how I have described him in the book. In the same way that Mrs Hudson will always be Rosalie Williams in my mind's eye.

I did make a mistake though, which I'm kicking myself for now. I have called the place at the Diogenes where speaking is allowed the 'Speaking Room' whereas it is actually the 'Stranger's Room'. Hopefully people will forgive me that small but understandable error.

So in this story we are treated to experiencing both Holmes and Mycroft setting their minds to a problem and watching them both compete in a little exercise of observation.

The tale of a Greek interpreter who is taken hostage and forced to help extract compliance from a Greek man who's sister is being forced into a marriage, is quite dark and doesn't really reach a full conclusion. It feels more like a vehicle to introduce Mycroft than anything else but is gripping all the same.

This one has to score highly but more for Mycroft than anything else – 8 out of 10.

Well, I don't know if it's because it's wages day again and my brain is too full of figures and pay-rates, but I can't think of much to say about this one.

I'm sure there are many Holmesian scholars who could write pages about this story; a neat little tale which involves a naval treaty that is stolen from the foreign office by the soon-to-be brother-in-law of an old school friend of Watson's who works there. I guess this is one of those times when I think to myself, – 'What are you doing? Who are you to write a blog about Sherlock Homes when you are not exactly an expert, just an ordinary admirer who has always enjoyed reading the stories? Is that really enough to qualify you for this task?'

But then husband comes to the rescue and reminds me that I have written a very well researched novel involving Holmes and couldn't possibly have got this far with my blogging adventure if I didn't know at least a little bit of what I was talking about.

This is very nice of him, though a little biased, but still doesn't help me think of much to say about the Naval Treaty except that it is rather long (like my day has been) for a short story and Holmes does an excellent job of wrapping things up when all seems hopeless. And, it is another case which Watson brings to him, like with the Engineer's Thumb, making him more than just a passive observer. Oh, and there is the mention of

Watson's moustache which is interesting because I couldn't remember there ever being one in the original stories and have therefore often wondered why people always portray him has having one. Well, now I know.

In my own my own novel, I have left it up to the reader's imagination by not stating either way about the good doctor's facial hair. In my mind's eye I pictured him as clean-shaven most of the time while writing it, and then seeing Jude Law with a 'tash was enough to seal the deal – sorry Jude, no offense intended.

Nothing wrong with the story at all really, it just didn't have enough about it to fully drag my mind away from a hard day at work. 5 out of 10.

This story is of such importance that I feel overwhelmed by the enormity of the task.

Well, where to start? I suppose it's best to start with Moriarty himself as he appears for the first time in this story. And with this I have a bit of a problem. It just feels a bit hurried, like Conan Doyle had decided to finish off Sherlock Holmes and needed to quickly invent a villain suitable for such a task.

Why haven't we heard of him before? If Moriarty was truly working away in the background for all those years doing his villainy, why is this the first time Holmes mentions him? And the other problem, which readers of my previous blogs will know, is that I find the description of Moriarty's inclination towards criminality very simplistic. To say, as Holmes does, that he has, 'Hereditary tendencies of the most diabolical kind' and 'a criminal strain ran in his blood', is very naive. Surely someone who has studied criminality in as much detail as Holmes would know that such things are not hereditary.

So what really did turn the brilliant maths professor to crime? Well, I have tried to answer this very comprehensively in my novel and it is based around the idea that he is an autistic savant.

There is much evidence to support this in the original text, such as his, 'Phenomenal mathematical ability', the way that 'He does little himself' and stays withdrawn from society instead paying and facilitating others to do the criminal acts for him. Even the curiously oscillating head could be seen as a sort of twitch, or compulsion. I have tried to flesh-out and give much more detail to this fascinating man and create a back-story to fill in the blanks left by the Final Problem.

As to the rest of the story, it does all feel a little hurried to me but is still gripping, clever and actually rather emotional. The devotion which Watson shows is touching, and I remember how well David Burke portrayed this in the Granada adaptation. I must also mention how fantastic I thought the characterisation of Moriarty was in BBC's Sherlock – making him into a playful, flirty, camp, but deadly villain was a stroke of absolute genius in my opinion. I do hope to send the creators a copy of my book and will post up a blog with their feedback if they are kind enough to submit any and happy for me to do so.

I admit that during the writing of Barefoot, I pictured Moriarty as being a curious mix of Eric Porter, who played the character so well in the Granada version, and Mr Burns from the Simpsons (though obviously not yellow) with his bird-like features and domed forehead. That particular combination seemed to work quite well for me.

My own novel includes The Final Problem in great detail and I have tried to stick to the movements in the original as much as possible, just adding in my own characters and weaving it into my own narrative. Holmes is working with the French Government and the adventure starts in Narbonne, the very place which Holmes writes to Watson from in the original. I hope this section of my book is a good example of where the astute Holmes fans will spot many original references such as getting the continental express from Victoria and disembarking at Canterbury, to the argument in the Strasbourg sale-a-manger when Holmes warns of the dangers ahead and expresses his desire to travel on alone. But, but by adding a new take on the proceedings and a back-story which explains so much, I hope new readers will enjoy it too whilst Holmes fans will appreciate the detail included and the way this has been adapted into something new whilst retaining elements of the original.

I spent so many hours slaving over this and my Penguin Complete Sherlock Holmes has so many notes, underlining, highlighting and drawings on the pages of The Final Problem that they are now almost impossible to read. But, re-read it I have, and I must admit that it remains very enjoyable (especially as we know it isn't really the end) and absorbing. Though how it must have felt to those reading it when it was first published and there was no hope at that point of a return, I can only imagine.

8.5 out of 10. Despite all the good points and obvious significance it still felt a bit rushed and underdeveloped.

It's back to business as Holmes returns from the dead to a very forgiving Doctor Watson.

If one of my very best friends had faked their own death, withheld the truth from me, and left me to mourn them for three years, I would be pretty annoyed if they suddenly turned up on my doorstep asking to renew acquaintances. But Watson is just so happy to see his friend alive that he doesn't really question Holmes' explanation that if Watson had known the truth he would surely have let it slip somehow. That's not showing much faith in the man who regularly dropped everything to accompany Holmes into dangerous and very sensitive situations without ever failing him or betraying a trust.

Add in the fact that Watson had suffered a genuine bereavement during Holmes' absence, presumably that of his first wife, and you can't help but feel sad for the doctor as he was alone during the period when he probably needed Holmes the most. The one time when Watson could have really used a friend, and the person who could have been the most comfort to him stayed away, even though he had somehow learned of the sad news.

Can we forgive Holmes for not trusting Watson? For letting him believe in a lie and mourn needlessly? Well, obviously we can because we are just so glad to have him back.

So off we go on another adventure just like old times and there is something quite satisfying and reassuring about this. The last of Moriarty's henchman is captured in the form of Colonel Moran and Holmes cleverly uses a wax bust of himself positioned by the window of his rooms at 221b to trap him. The story is very imaginative and does neatly tie up all the loose ends.

Once again, I have used the Empty House heavily in my own novel and it's another part of my Penguin Complete Sherlock Holmes which is covered in notes and underlining. I have, once again, stuck very closely to the original but this time there has been some very significant changes in Watson's life and only he knows the truth. For once, Holmes is in the dark and this threatens to change the dynamic of their friendship forever.

Re-reading the original has reminded me of why I called the poisoner, who features in the 'Paris' part of Barefoot, Morgan. It is because when Holmes goes to his index of Biographies to look up Moran he mentions Morgan the poisoner. I do hope fellow Holmes fans spot that one.

And another curious thing that springs into my memory is that of the confusion over Moriarty's first name. In the Empty House he is referred to as James, but in the Final Problem his brother is called James. Can it be that both children were given the same name? That must have been confusing when they were growing up. This did cause me some angst when writing about Moriarty's childhood and I eventually decided that both boys

71

were probably given the same name as their father but while the eldest continued to use it, the youngest was commonly known by a different name. Conan Doyle really did get mixed up over names didn't he?

Though the explanation for Holmes' reappearance feels a little hurried and unrealistic, the story that follows is enjoyable and it is great to have Holmes and Watson re-united and back on form together. Normality is thankfully restored - 7 out of 10.

56 Stories in 56 Days – The Adventure of the Norwood Builder

Doyle himself lived at Norwood for four years.

During this time, Doyle completed the compilation of stories which make up The Adventures of Sherlock Holmes and made the decision to 'kill off' his most famous creation. London historian and Holmesian scholar Alistair Duncan wrote an excellent book on this period of Doyle's life called The Norwood Author which won the Howlett Literary Award this year, 2011.

Back to the original story and the fascinating details it reveals about the relationship between Holmes and Watson after the detective returns 'from the dead' and is back with his old friend.

At Holmes' request, Watson sells his practice to a mysterious doctor Verner and returns to live in his old rooms at Baker Street.

As if this isn't quite extraordinary enough, we then learn that Verner is actually a relative of Holmes and paid a generous amount for the practice because it was actually Holmes who put up the money himself. Gosh, for a man that is supposed to be without emotion, this is a very clear statement of deep emotional attachment towards his friend and how much he needs him. But there are alternate views to be considered – could it have been guilt that prompted such generosity? Did Holmes feel guilty about leaving Watson to mourn him for three years, putting him through all that grief and not being there to support him when his wife died? And what about all the money Watson has lost over the years due to neglecting his business and chasing off after Holmes? That trip to Switzerland must have been very expensive, not to mention earlier examples such as rushing from London to Lyon in twenty-four hours to be at Holmes' bedside when he fell ill there. Was this money his compensation? A thank you and a sorry which Holmes couldn't find the words to say in the conventional way? Or was it simply an act of love?

As to the rest of the story, it returns us to the tried and tested formula of an innocent man being arrested and the evidence stacking up against him, with Holmes trying to prove his innocence much to the amazement of Inspector Lestrade who teases him as every fresh piece of evidence comes to light in the apparent favour of the Inspector's case.

Unusually, Holmes works on intuition at the start of the investigation. I say unusual because what tends to differentiate between Holmes and other detectives is his method, the reasoned observation which he uses to form his opinion, but in this case it is the other way around and he looks for evidence to fit his theory.

A young lawyer is accused of murdering a builder who had once been a suitor of his mother's until she threw him over in favour of another. Mr Jonas Oldacre turns up at the young man's office and asks him to draw up his will, in which the lawyer will be his heir. When Mr Oldacre is believed to have been murdered and his body burned in a fire the night the lawyer visits him to conclude their business, there is only one suspect.

Holmes very cleverly discovers that the builder faked his death and is still hiding in the house – in a den of his own construction. To take a little revenge on Lestrade who had teased him so much for being supposedly on the wrong track, Holmes dramatically gets the builder to run out from his hiding place after a cry of "Fire" is given by Holmes, Watson, Lestrade and the sceptical policemen. Lestrade is suitably humbled and an innocent man saved.

Brilliant, what a great story full of humour, friendship, intrigue and deduction. 9 out of 10.

56 Stories in 56 Days – The Adventure of the Dancing Men

The Dancing Men is one of my favourite stories.

The story begins with Holmes demonstrating how well he knows his old friend by once again seeming to read his mind and remarking that it is clear Watson has decided not to invest in South African securities.

He explains his simple deductions to an astonished Watson and shows us once again the intimate knowledge he has of his housemate down to knowing who he plays billiards with and the fact that Holmes keeps Watson's 'check' book (note the curious spelling Doyle used) safely locked in his drawer because the good doctor can't be trusted to be sensible with it. What a lovely friendship they have come to share by this point.

Holmes has shown his hand by asking Watson to move back in with him and Watson has acknowledged the void in his life which he experienced after Holmes' 'death' in Switzerland. There is inter-dependency between them which I think both have come to recognise and accept.

Holmes passes over to Watson a piece of paper with what appears to be a child's drawing on it comprising a set of matchstick figures who appear to be dancing. It is actually a cipher sent to the wife of a Norfolk squire by an old love from Chicago who has tracked her down to England in order to win her back. He was a member of a ruthless criminal gang and she was the boss' daughter who fled to escape his wrong-doings. The lover ends up shooting the new husband and the wife tries to shoot herself.

What starts out as quite light-hearted becomes rather dark. And yet again love and romance plays a major part in the drama as does the tried and tested formula of someone having a past from overseas (usually the colonies somewhere) which comes back to haunt them, often in the form of a past love. This is why I find it so easy to get the stories confused with one another as there is such a thread of commonality which runs through them.

Anyway, Holmes is brought the mysterious drawings by his client, the lady's husband, but he delays in travelling to Norfolk and ultimately feels guilty that he may have been able to prevent the tragedy which followed if he had acted sooner.

This is the only fault he makes in an otherwise brilliant investigation – particularly the deciphering of the dancing men which is simply genius, though made to look so simple once he explains it.

I have read this story many times but here again I couldn't put it down – 9 out of 10.

56 stories in 56 days – The Adventure of the Solitary Cyclist

The story centres on the experiences of a Miss Violet Smith – not to be confused with Violet Hunter from The Copper Beeches.

Miss Smith makes quite an impression on Watson who clearly had a bit of a fancy for her - 'Young and beautiful woman, tall, graceful and queenly,' is his emotive description.

Holmes is initially too busy to investigate the strange case of Miss Smith being followed by a mysterious man as she cycles into town from Farnham to visit her mother from the country house where she was employed as a music teacher. Instead Holmes sends Watson to investigate and is pretty scathing about his results. Watson is happy to tootle off and do Holmes' bidding, but then what else has he to do now that he is no longer practicing medicine?

So even though their friendship has deepened of late, Holmes can still be very insensitive towards Watson, not to mention quite bossy. But then, I guess he has every right to ask favours after paying above the odds for Watson's medical practice, even though Watson is probably still unaware that it was actually Holmes who put up the money.

The adventure itself is fairly straightforward and doesn't contain many opportunities for brilliant deduction. And yet again it involves people from abroad with dodgy intentions. If I wasn't so stupidly busy at the moment I'd go through all the stories and work out how many of the villains are foreign and how many are English, I'm guessing the majority are from distant shores.

I felt it was a bit of a come-down after the Dancing Men, which is a hard act to follow, so it gets 6 out of 10.

Ok, perhaps Reginald Musgrave wasn't the best client name after all, now that Thorneycroft Huxtable has stepped into the frame.

The big man turns up at 221b and promptly faints with the stress of the situation he is bringing to Holmes. This is followed by a great line from Watson – 'We stared in silent amazement at this ponderous piece of wreckage, which told of some sudden and fatal storm far out on the ocean of life'.

This is then followed by another clever line as Watson takes the man's pulse – 'With my finger on the thready pulse, where the stream of life trickled thin and small'. Once again, Conan Doyle reminds us what a skilful wordsmith he was and how such lines elevate the stories to a more literary level, beyond that of a simple crime drama.

Mr Huxtable regains his senses and asks not for a brandy or a smoke to calm his nerves, but a glass of milk and a biscuit. What a great choice, clearly a man after my own heart. There's not much in life that can't be made a little better with the enjoyment of a nice biscuit. Preferably a custard cream in my opinion. I had an assistant one Christmas at the office who realised that the best way to get me back on track after a staffing calamity, usually a temp not turning up for work and an angry client calling to demand a replacement, was to push a tray of biscuits under my nose and let me munch my way through. She brought in a selection every morning for that very purpose.

Unusually in this story, Holmes is prompted into action by the promise of a reward of six thousand pounds if he can find the missing only son of the Duke of Holdernesse, the ten year old Lord Saltire who has disappeared from the Priory prep school where Mr Huxtable is the principal. He is reluctant to act until a reward is mentioned.

Taking Watson with him, Holmes travels to Mackleton to try and unravel the mystery. This mainly involves some clever analysis of bicycle tracks and a revelation that Holmes is an expert on tire treads (42 different impressions to be exact) as well as the tobacco and footprints which we already know about. Holmes energetically bounces around the local countryside following tracks and clues and eventually finds the boy concealed at a local inn.

It is no surprise to me that the somewhat shady private secretary of the Duke's is behind the matter and this is another of those rare occasions when I could guess 'whodunit' ahead of Holmes. What I didn't work out was why and that is where the story does become a bit unbelievable for me. The private secretary is actually the Duke's illegitimate son and he has arranged for the boy to be taken so that he can blackmail the Duke into making him the sole heir instead. All well and good except for the fact that the Duke has already discovered this three days prior to Holmes' arrival and agrees to leave his young son with the captors for reasons I don't fully understand and to save the skin of his illegitimate boy.

Holmes makes sure the Duke writes out the cheque for the reward money before revealing that he knows the truth and is clearly very happy to have taken such a sum. This is unusual behaviour from Holmes, but then as the client is such a rich man, who can blame him for taking the spoils? And that really was a massive amount of money back then, considering that a good yearly wage was a hundred pounds. As Watson isn't working at this time, Holmes is the only bread-winner and I'm sure this 'bread' will easily settle their rent for many years to come.

It's always enjoyable to read of Holmes being so on form and the story does not disappoint in this sense at all, though I do have some issues with the plot regarding the actions of the father towards his vulnerable ten-year-old son and the cruelty of the elder son towards his half-brother – surely he didn't think he could get away with that in the end?

7 out of 10

* By my reckoning we're halfway through now. Thanks for reading so far.

By this point in his career, Holmes has found fame, success and also wealth thanks to that cheque from Lord Holdernesse.

But as Watson reminds us, these things are not the focus of Holmes' work and despite his great success he still turns down cases that are not of interest even though the financial gains would be high and clients notorious. He hasn't risen too high to take on cases where the only reward is the resolution to a fascinating problem and remains happy for the local police to take the credit for his discoveries.

In this story we are introduced to a young police inspector, Hopkins, who is very respectful towards Holmes and seems keen to learn from so great a teacher. Holmes in turn has high regard for the potential of this young man. But still, the outcome is the same as with Lestrade and all the other police who work with Holmes – Hopkins fixes upon the wrong theory and ignores the hints from Holmes which would put him back on the right track.

In Watson's introduction we hear about how Holmes has been to the local butchers with a harpoon and tried to drive it through a hanging pig carcass. Nothing unusual there then. This is followed by a hearty breakfast and a visit from Hopkins during which he explains the details of the case. An old sea captain, Black Peter, who was a hateful drunkard, has been murdered in his funny little cabin by someone who stabbed him with his own harpoon.

The strength needed to drive the harpoon through the man's body, the initials on a pouch of ship's tobacco (the dead man didn't smoke much) and the presence of two glasses and a bottle of rum on the table suggest straight away to Holmes that the murderer must be a sailor. He busies himself following this line of inquiry by taking on the persona of Captain Basil who advertises for a harpooner to join an expedition. All great fun – particularly at the expense of Hopkins.

Hopkins has arrested an innocent young man who has got caught up the case due to something complicated involving his father and some investments which the murdered man stole from him.

Holmes reminds us all, and young Hopkins, why he is the master of his profession and as usual, makes everything seem so obvious once explained.

Holmes curiously remarks at the end that he and Watson will be going to Norway, presumably for a holiday but this seems very out of character. The innocent man's father was killed by Black Peter in that area but I don't see any professional reason why Holmes would go there unless I have missed something. So perhaps, due to his heavily workload of late and all that money from Lord Holdernese, now seems like the perfect time to take a break – and how nice to take Watson along too? I hope he pays for everything though, as poor Watson is now his full-time helper and without income.

7 out of 10.

56 Stories in 56 Days – The Adventure of Charles Augustus Milverton

Well, I suppose this story is where my personal literary adventure really began.

When I was sixteen, I wrote a full-length Sherlock Holmes screenplay which was a sequel to the Granada dramatization of this story. It was quite an achievement for my age and I worked on it for many a long hour, even using a home-writing course to learn all about how to correctly write scripts for TV with the technical stage directions and other requirements. It was very simplistic and involved Milverton coming back from the dead to seek revenge on Holmes in ghostly form. I do cringe now at the naivety of it, but the process did spark up an enjoyment of writing about Sherlock Holmes which ultimately led to the creation of my first published novel, Barefoot on Baker Street.

So I owe a lot to this story and it was a pleasure to re-read it now. I suppose the key points of interest are that Holmes actually breaks the law by breaking into Milverton's house and accessing the safe so that he can burn all the incriminating letters. He then stands back and watches as one of Milverton's victims murders him in cold blood. Holmes keeps this truth from the police to protect the lady.

This does sound rather extraordinary but we have seen before how Holmes uses his own judgement in exercising justice and takes full advantage of being an unofficial person. We have also seen how he can feel strong, emotional revulsion against certain villains and great sympathy for the victims. It also demonstrates Watson's devotion to Holmes as he too colludes in this law-breaking without question.

This is the story in which Holmes becomes engaged to Milverton's maid in order to gain information about the house in the disguise of a plumber. He walks out with her each evening and they talk – 'Those talks! However, I have got all I wanted'.

Clearly such a romantic action was not to his taste, but then perhaps he just made this remark for affect to Watson. What if Holmes did actually quite enjoy those intimate walks with a devoted young girl upon his arm? I would more readily see him fall in love with a savvy maid than a lady. Did he kiss her I wonder? Surely you wouldn't have become engaged to a man, even back then, without even a brief kiss?

Watson is rightly shocked by Holmes' deception of the young lady but Holmes does assure him that there is another more worthy suitor waiting in the wings to take over when he disappears. I still do think his actions are unfair but I suppose justified in light of the villain he faces and the high stakes if he fails.

In the opening part of the story Holmes refers to CAM as 'The worst man in London', and this hatred only deepens as the story continues. Even Watson is shocked as Holmes goes on to describe the cruel and villainous business in which CAM distinguished himself – 'I had seldom heard my friend speak with such intensity of feeling'.

Milverton made his living from acquiring sensitive letters from crooked maids, footmen, valets, anyone with something incriminating to sell. He would then, when the moment was right, blackmail his helpless victims mercilessly and the law could do nothing to stop him.

Milverton is a brilliantly devised baddie, I would even argue that he is more convincing and better described than Moriarty. And the Granada episode was one of my favourites with CAM played to perfection by Robert Hardy.

Brilliant, love it, even though a conclusion isn't brought about by any particularly brilliant deduction by Holmes but sometimes it's good to see him get his hands dirty in this way. And what a great villain we have in Milverton, definitely my favourite baddie of all the stories. 10 out of 10.

What a treat it has been re-reading The Return as it contains so many of my favourites, including this great little story.

I really love The Six Napoleons and think it contains everything which makes a Holmes story great. There is humour, action, friendship and Inspector Lestrade getting things wrong as usual. Though this time, the Inspector is truly humbled and astonished when Holmes reveals the truth and both he and Watson burst into spontaneous applause. Holmes is touched by the response causing Watson to comment – 'It was at such moments that for an instant he ceased to be a reasoning machine, and betrayed his human love for admiration and applause.'

Lestrade is so overwhelmed by Holmes' dramatic smashing of the Napoleon bust and how he then pulls out the black pearl, that he makes a rather lovely statement – 'We're not jealous of you at Scotland Yard. No sir, we are very proud of you!'

He goes on to say that if Holmes were to come to the station the following day there is not a person there who would not wish to shake his hand and Watson tells us – 'It seemed to me that he was more nearly moved by the softer human emotions than I had ever seen him'.

It does seem to me throughout The Return, that Holmes has become increasingly human and less machine-like. I think that by living with Watson and working so closely with him during this period, Watson has softened Holmes. To the point where I would argue that even Lestrade has become a friend of sorts, especially as we learn at the start of this story how he regularly calls around to 221b of an evening for a chat.

The story is simple enough, an Italian wrong 'un is in possession of a stolen precious pearl and gets arrested by the police over another matter. At the time of his arrest he rushes into a factory where he used to work as a sculptor and pushes the pearl into the wet clay of a bust of Napoleon. He is imprisoned for a year and on his release sets about tracking down the bust, which was one of six that have been sold all over London by now. He finds out who they have been sold to and breaks in to their houses to get at the busts.

The police seize upon the burglaries and smashed busts presuming it to be the work of a madman with a hatred of Napoleon. Holmes finds out the truth in a most workman like fashion which is simply brilliant and a joy to follow. He works out where the final bust is and writes to the owner expressing his desire to purchase it. The man brings the object to 221b and Holmes smashes it in front of his appreciative audience. It's the simplicity; the neatness of this story which I think makes it so good.

I seem to remember that the Basil Rathbone episode of this story was one of the best and did stick quite closely to the original. And why not, as I don't see any way of improving upon it. Has to be another 10 out of 10.

All I could remember about this one was that it had something to do with pencils.

Mr Hilton Soames, a tutor and lecturer at an unspecified university, comes to see Holmes in the hope that he can find out which of three students could have gained access to his room and copied a Greek passage which was to be translated as part of an exam.

Holmes and Watson happened to be staying at the university town due to other business and this is just the sort of strange little problem Holmes loves to solve – no actual crime, no reward, no celebrity client, just a situation which is beyond everyone else and seemingly impossible.

This provides the perfect opportunity for him to show off and apply his unique skills.

Once in the lecturer's room, Holmes finds pencil sharpenings and from this can determine the maker and the size. There is also a curious lump of clay with sawdust shavings mixed in. He finds a second one in the bedroom and it becomes clear that the person hid in there when the lecturer came back unexpectedly.

To cut a rather long story short the culprit is the sport student and the clay was from the long jump pit. The spikes on his shoes and his natural height allowed him to see into the room and noticed the exam papers on the table.

This is one of my husband's favourite stories but I'm not so keen and I don't really know why. There is plenty of that clever deduction we all love but it just doesn't capture me for some reason. Perhaps it is because Holmes is grumpy again – Watson tells us that he is agitated being away from Baker Street and his messy rooms with all his paraphernalia inside. He doesn't really include Watson in the investigation and goes off alone to pursue his ideas saying - "Not one of your cases, Watson – mental, not physical".

This seems rather unfair and disappointing considering how close they have become lately – 6 out of 10.

56 stories in 56 days – The Adventure of the Golden Pince-Nez

Interestingly, Watson refers to "our work" at the start of this one.

Watson writes: "When I look at the three manuscript volumes which contain **our work** for the year 1894 . . ." Clearly the business has become more of a joint venture now that Watson devotes his full-time energies to it. They must both now live off the proceeds because Watson no longer has his medical practice. It's an interesting quote because Watson certainly wouldn't have referred to it as "our work" in the early days of their union. We also hear that Holmes won an autographed letter of thanks from the French President and the Order of the Legion of Honour. Wow, impressive stuff. Business has improved greatly now that Watson is back at 221b.

Hopkins appears again in this story, the young detective in which Holmes has great hope for the future. He freely admits to Holmes that he can't make "Neither head nor tail" of the murder of Professor Coram's secretary Mr Willoughby Smith at Yoxley Old Place. A golden pince-nez was found in the hand of the dead man and Holmes does his usual startling piece of analysis describing perfectly the features of the woman who was wearing them. Another apparently innocuous object also yields a massive clue when Holmes works out that without her pince-nez the lady would have become confused by the cocanut (sic) matting and lost her way, following it into the professor's bedroom. Therefore he must be hiding her.

By smoking heavily and dropping lots of ash near the suspected hiding place, Holmes was able to return to the room and see that the ash had been disturbed as the person came out from their hiding place behind the bookcase.

It turns out that the professor is not English, but Russian, and the woman is his estranged wife. Yet again, mistakes of the past come back to haunt, but this time an innocent young man was the victim as the professor's wife accidentally stabbed him when he caught her trying to take things from the bureau.

An interesting story, but a rather sad conclusion as the woman takes her own life. In the Granada episode, the professor is murdered in the end by a member of the Russian brotherhood who he wronged, but in the original he is the only one who survives.

I think I prefer the TV ending as this one feels a little incomplete to me. For that reason it's a 6 out of 10.

56 stories in 56 days – The Adventure of the Missing Three-Quarter

There is a period of inactivity and Watson fears that Holmes may turn to drugs.

Watson tells us that over the years he has managed to wean Holmes off drugs but as there has been a sustained period without work, he fears there will be a relapse. As I have said before in previous blogs, I don't think Holmes used drugs because he was bored, but because his mental processes could overwhelm him if he had nothing to channel them into – like voices he needed to drown out.

But Watson takes a rather more conventional view and is relieved when a case comes their way in the form of a missing rugby player. I confess I had no idea what a three-quarter was and presumed it was a coin of some sort when I first read this story. Holmes didn't have the foggiest either when team captain Cyril Overton started wittering on about Godfrey Staunton, the famous rugby player who has disappeared the day before a crucial match with Oxford. Surprised at Holmes' ignorance he exclaims: "Good Lord! Mr Holmes, where have you lived?"
My husband regularly says things like that to me when his sporting talk is met with a blank expression.

This is a very enjoyable story and Holmes comes up against a worthy adversary in the form of the sinister Dr Armstrong who he states could even fill the gap left by the late

Professor Moriarty, if he so inclined. But, actually the doctor turns out to be the hero of the story protecting the missing young man's secret wife who sadly dies at the end of the tale, with the rugby player weeping at her bedside.

It is a clever writer who can take you from humour to tragedy as smoothly as Conan Doyle does. On the one hand you have the comical Cyril Overton and his boisterous rugby talk, the brilliant use of Pompey the sniffer dog and, of course, the hilarious old miser Lord Mount-James, the missing boy's only relative and the reason for the concealment of his marriage. But then we discover the sad young death at the end and everything takes on a deeper meaning.

A simple but clever story with a great twist that draws you in very quickly and doesn't quite let you go for some time afterwards – well worth 7 out of 10.

Holmes has an epic moan at Watson on the way to the scene of the crime.

On the way to Abbey Grange, Holmes has a massive moan at poor Watson about his literary shortcomings. He really does go on and on about it to the point where Watson snaps – "Why do you not write them yourself?" with some bitterness. Holmes is oblivious to the hurt in this comment and continues to witter on about how he intends to but not until his declining years. They then start to discuss the current case concerning the murder of Lord Eustace Brackenstall. If I were Watson, considering Holmes had turned him out of bed and whisked him off at such an early hour without breakfast, I would have demanded an apology for such rudeness before a subject change. But then, I am a nightmare in the mornings, especially if I haven't had breakfast.

Here again we have a highly-spirited wife from overseas. Her husband, Lord Eustace Brackenstall, was a violent drunkard and has been murdered. Suspicion initially falls on a gang of local burglars known to the police, but Holmes senses a different explanation. Due to the knots with which the lady was tied to a chair and the nimble way someone climbed up to the bell rope, he suspects a sailor and, indeed, the guilty man is one who the lady met on her voyage over to England from Australia. He is in love with her and acts in defence of her and himself when he strikes her violent husband with a poker.

Here again we see Holmes hide the truth from the police, even his young prodigy Hopkins, to protect the man who, he feels, deserves to go free. The advantages of being an unofficial person are clear once again, though I don't see how this one could stay hidden for long. Where would that leave Holmes if the truth eventually came out? I think this is the biggest risk he has taken of all the times when he has kept the truth to himself. Still it's a 7 out of 10.

There is a confusing chronology about this one.

It is not clear when Watson is writing the Second Stain or when the events actually occurred. All we know is that this is meant to be the last published account of Holmes' work because he has now retired to his cottage on the Sussex Downs and 'Notoriety has become hateful to him'. So what has happened to Watson by this point? We knew that Holmes asked him to move back to Baker Street after his re-appearance from the dead and that Watson sold his medical practise, so what did he do when Holmes retired? Perhaps the answers will become clearer as we work though the next compilation – His Last Bow. They certainly don't present themselves in this tale.

Holmes gives his permission to Watson for this story to be published only because it is the most important international case he has ever solved. And the client is the Prime Minister of England no less!

The drama centres on a letter from a foreign royal personage who fired off an angry, hot-headed, note about British colonial interests in a moment of madness which, if made public, could result in war between the two countries. It is stolen from the despatch-box of the Right-Honourable Trelawney Hope, Secretary for European Affairs. Through various twists and turns, it becomes clear to Holmes that it is Mrs Hope who has taken the letter and persuades her to return it to her husband's despatch-box before any harm is done. Watson spends a whole paragraph describing her beauty and has evidently developed a bit of a crush – bless him.

We don't know the date when the incidents took place as Watson wanted to be discrete, but as he is living at Baker Street it must be either in the early days of his association with Holmes or when he returned to live in his old rooms after the Empty House. I would argue it would more likely be the latter as Holmes' reputation in the early days would not have been strong enough to secure the trust of the Prime Minister.

It's so strange to think of Holmes as retired, tatting around with his bees all alone. And this image is juxtaposed with the energetic Holmes in this story – running around London for days chasing up leads, barely eating or sleeping, turning up back at home looking moody and scrapping away on his violin before dashing off out again and ultimately, triumphantly, gaining high praise from the Prime Minister.

Holmes remains un-phased by the importance of his client and stands up to the premier during their initial meeting when he refuses to reveal the contents of the letter. Holmes makes it clear that he would rather walk away from such a high-profile case than not be trusted completely. And ultimately, he does his usual trick of choosing to keep secrets himself in order to protect the foreign secretary's wife and avoid a scandal.

It is certainly a case of great international importance and a satisfying example of Holmes at his best, but personally I prefer the smaller, but more unusual cases such as The Six Napoleons. However, I certainly did enjoy following Holmes on this case as he shone light into what appeared to be total, and impossible, darkness. A well-deserved 8 out of 10.

56 Stories in 56 Days – The Adventure of Wisteria Lodge

This is the first story in the compilation titled 'His Last Bow' and starts with a brief description of Holmes' current situation.

Watson tells us that Holmes is alive and well, though occasionally troubled by bouts of rheumatism. He is living on a small farm upon the Downs near Eastbourne enjoying his retirement. The story of Wisteria Gables pre-dates this and is set in 1892. I feel somewhat let down by the story. I want to hear more about Holmes' retirement and why he has let Watson continue to write about him when The Second Stain was meant to be the last time. What has happened to Watson once Holmes has retired? Has he gone back to medical work? Has he remarried? I have tried to look at some of these things in my own novel, and interestingly have named the house in which Watson ultimately ends up living as Wisteria Gables – a mix of Wisteria Lodge and The Three Gables.

This story is really not one of my favourites, too long and complicated in my opinion.

It's basically a tale, inexplicably split into two parts, about a nasty dictator who fled from his country taking great wealth with him and goes to hide in England. A gang have been following him trying to seek revenge and some of its members are staying in a nearby house.

They enlist the services of a woman whose husband was killed by the dictator and she gains employment in his household as a nanny. Here's where the problems start for me – why didn't she just kill him herself as she hated him so much? Why did they wait so long to make the attack? Anyway, the leader of the gang befriends a respectable fellow and arranges for him to stay at his house, changing the times on the clocks so that he can provide an alibi, but the dictator gets wind of the planed attack and kills his would-be murder first. Gosh, it is far too much coming-and-going for a short story.

For once, the police are on the right track, and the promising Inspector Baynes reaches the same conclusion as Holmes. This is a first, a big change from all previous stories.

Holmes is able to deliver the crucial witness, the nanny, but still justice cannot be done as the villain escapes. There is a report years later which tells of his eventual murder but the whole thing seems unfinished to me.

I didn't enjoy this one and wanted to know more about the central characters rather than some bonkers dictator. It's a 4 out of 10 I'm afraid – here's hoping that the rest of His Last Bow scores a little better.

The beginning of this story is giving me a strange sense of deja vu.

Let me explain, or try to at least. There is a passage at the start of The Cardboard Box which is exactly the same in the Resident Patient. Confused? Well this is the reason – as far as I understand it anyway.

The Cardboard Box was originally supposed to be included in The Memoirs, but Conan Doyle decided to leave it out due to some sexual content. It was presumed that the story would therefore never be published. It seemed to be very unfortunate that the brilliant piece of deduction which Holmes does at the start involving knowing Watson's innermost thoughts just by reading his body language, would never be seen. So it was decided to insert this into the Resident Patient instead. Eventually though, the Cardboard Box, minus the sexual bit, was published as part of His Last Bow and the duplication occurred. Clear? I know, all a bit strange and I probably haven't explained it very well. And I wonder what the sexual content was? It would be very interesting to know what Doyle regarded as inappropriate.

The story itself is a rather gruesome one about an enraged husband who murders his wife and her lover, cuts off an ear from each of them, and sends them to his sister-in-law who he holds responsible for turning his wife against him. The ears are accidently received by the third sister who calls in the police. As usual, Lestrade gets it completely wrong and it is left to Holmes to find out the truth behind the unpleasant parcel.

An analysis of the string which binds it and the knot suggests a sailor is to blame. Discovering that the male ear had a hole for a piercing also compounded the sailor theory. The female ear was remarkably similar to that of the lady who received it suggesting that she must be related to the victim, and quite closely. Holmes professed to have made a study into ears – 'Each ear is as a rule quite distinctive and differs from all other ones. In last year's Anthropological Journal you will find two short monographs from my pen on the subject'. There really is no limit to the strange bits of knowledge which Holmes would store in his great brain!

A photograph in the lady's house of herself with two sisters prompts Holmes to inquire whether either of them is married to a sailor and indeed one of them is – a nasty drunkard. Hey presto, mystery solved.

That usual happy blend of observation, clever logic and sound reasoning gives Holmes all the answers.

An enjoyable story, but with a sad ending and macabre undertones – 7 out of 10.

This is another complicated story, but unlike Wisteria Lodge, I think it hangs together really well.

Landlady Mrs Warren comes to see Holmes regarding her unusual lodger. This strange man took the room, paid above the odds on the condition she left him completely alone, and he hasn't left the room or been seen for the last ten days – except going out on the evening he arrived and returning after everyone had gone to bed.

Holmes is busy at the time when she calls, sticking things in his scrap book, and is initially rather rude and dismissive towards her. Mrs Warren persists and persuades him with a little flattery. Watson tells us –'Holmes was accessible upon the side of flattery, and also, to do him justice, upon the side of kindliness'. It is something that this blogging project has reminded me of – that Holmes was capable of much kindness, sensitivity, even emotion at times and the stereotype of a cold, clinical thinking machine is far too simplistic.

The lodger who stays in the room is not actually the person who engaged it. There was a switch and the person occupying the room is actually an Italian woman who is hiding from the leader of The Red Circle – an Italian mafia-style gang of which her husband (who took the rooms initially) was a member. The couple fled to London in order to escape the gang because the leader, Gorgiano, made a pass at the wife then ordered her husband to murder a close family friend. Once in London, the husband hides his wife at Mrs Warren's for safety – that is why she hasn't seen her lodger leave the room for ten days.

The police are already investigating the situation with help from an American detective from Pinkerton's agency. Holmes' investigation interweaves with the official one and ultimately the woman's husband kills Gorgiano. Upon hearing the wife's story, all decide that he should not be punished as he was justified in bumping off such a notorious murderer and all-round nasty villain. So all's well that ends well and a complicated tale draws to a close.

Generally, I do prefer the more small-scale stories to these complicated international sagas, but there is a subtlety to this one which I enjoyed. 7 out of 10.

Holmes has a new hobby – music of the middle-ages – why? Why? Could he be any more extreme in his interests? And how unusual to find him studying so hard at something which doesn't relate to his work.

Normally, Holmes liked to keep his brain uncluttered and fill it only with relevant information, but then I guess music has always been an interesting exception to this.

The story reacquaints us with Mycroft Holmes, Sherlock's elder brother. We do gain some extra information about him this time. Holmes now felt able to trust Watson enough to tell him how indispensable Mycroft really was to the British government. Holmes says to Watson – "You would also be right in a sense if you had said that occasionally he *is* the British Government".

We hear more about the similarities between the brothers such as their singular devotion to their work, the orderly brains with fantastic memories for detailed facts and the lack of ambition they both share in terms of wanting fame or wealth.

Mycroft comes to visit Holmes and Watson, causing Holmes to remark that it is only the second time he has ever done so and the case he brings must be extremely important to make him break his routine. Mycroft is a stickler for routine – "Has his rails and he runs on them" as Holmes explains. So again we are (or I am certainly) reminded of all those peculiarities which correlate with symptoms of autism and savantism so clearly evident in the two brothers – the genetic connection only serves to prove the theory in my mind.

A young man called Cadogan West has been found dead on the underground. To my knowledge, this is the first time the underground has been mentioned in the stories as Holmes and Watson never seem to use it. I have always found this rather surprising and wonder why Doyle didn't ever see fit to include this great feat of engineering in the stories before. Anyway, Mycroft reveals that the young man was actually found to be in possession of vital Government papers which detailed the plans of the Bruce-Partington submarine. The three most important pages are missing and Mycroft wants Holmes to find them before they fall into the wrong hands.

This is another of those cases when all seems to be in darkness and you think to yourself – "How on earth is he going to sort this one out? It's impossible" and the resolution at the end when he does is all the greater for it.

Through his investigation Holmes discovers that Cadogan West is innocent and the papers were planted on him by the brother of a high-ranking civil servant and an international agent. He was about to expose them when they killed him and pushed his body out of a window and onto the roof of an underground carriage which paused below. When the carriage changes track further along, the body falls to the rails.

Holmes is simply brilliant in working all this out and the story is a perfect example of his method. And once again the benefits of being an unofficial person become clear when he breaks into the house of the suspect – no need to faff around waiting for a search warrant. It must be remembered that this does give Holmes a massive advantage over the police and allows him to do things they simply couldn't.

Holmes asks Watson to accompany him on the illegal house-breaking mission but Watson is reluctant at first. Holmes reminds him that this is an issue of national importance and Watson enthusiastically agrees to do his duty prompting Holmes to say – "I knew you would not shirk at the last". Watson then makes a lovely observation revealing so much about the depth of their friendship – 'I saw something in his eyes which was nearer to tenderness than I had ever seen'.

Considering Holmes has no other friends and this was only the second time his own brother had ever been to his house, he really must think a very great deal of Watson to be so attached to him.

At the end of the story we hear about Holmes receiving an emerald tie-pin, "From a certain gracious lady" who I presume is Queen Victoria herself. Though it is unusual for him to take gifts, you can quite understand him doing so on this occasion. Mycroft had made it clear that he could receive a title for his work on this case but Holmes' nature was such that he did not want that honour – the little tie-pin does seem a more appropriate gesture. What an adventure! 9 out of 10.

Well, where do you start with this one? I feel quite overwhelmed by the task in hand.

This story is interesting on two different levels. Firstly there is what actually happens, and secondly what this tells us about Holmes and his relationship with Watson.

Let's start with what happens. Holmes is on the trail of a botanist called Culverton Smith who is an expert on a particular tropical disease. Holmes knows that he poisoned a young man called Victor Savage by giving him the disease which led to his death but can't prove it. He cleverly concocts a plan to trap Culverton Smith into confessing in front of a witness – the starting point for which is a little wooden box with a spike inside sent to him by the botanist with the hope of infecting him.

Holmes realises that the box is dangerous and avoids infection, but decides to pretend that the plan worked in order to lure Culverton Smith to Baker Street and straight into his trap. Holmes goes without food or water for three days and uses stage make-up to make him look like he's only hours from death. Mrs Hudson fetches Watson who is horrified and genuinely moved by his friend's appearance. Holmes insists on being treated by Culverton Smith and sends Watson to fetch him, insisting that he travel back first.

At the last second, Holmes makes a startled Watson conceal himself behind the bed and so he hears when Culverton

Smith taunts Holmes (who he thinks is dying) about how he got away with the last murder and is about to get away with this one too.

Watson comes out from his hiding place and inspector Morton rushes into the room to apprehend the villain. That in itself is a great story, especially in the way it unfolds and we remain as in-the-dark as Watson until almost the end.

I remember the first time I read it and just couldn't put it down because I was utterly convinced Holmes really was dying and didn't suspect for one minute that he was faking it. There is just something refreshing and different about this one – it doesn't follow the usual pattern of a client turning up at 221b, telling their story and Holmes having to unravel the case. We come in on the investigation just before its conclusion which gives it a brisk feel.

The other level of interest is the love shown between Holmes and Watson as the latter tries to help his friend with such deep concern and the former in his sincere apologies for playing with Watson's emotions and being so very sharp with him at the start.

When trying to hurriedly get Watson to hide behind the bed, Holmes says – "Quick, man, if you love me!" – such a touching line as Watson clearly does very much. I believe this is reciprocated, shown strongly when Holmes sees Watson pick up the deadly little box not realising what it contained – 'It was a dreadful cry that he gave', Watson tells us, 'a yell which might have been heard down the street. My skin went cold and my hair bristled at that horrible scream. As I turned I caught a glimpse of a convulsed face and frantic eyes. I stood paralyzed, with the little box in my hand'.

We also hear from Watson a brief, and very humorous, description of what a terrible lodger Holmes was but that Mrs Hudson was very fond of him. We also hear that he paid 'princely' sums of rent as compensation to her and, 'The whole house might have been purchased at the price which Holmes paid for his rooms during the years that I was with him'.

Watson also comments on Holmes' attitude to women in general, saying that he 'Disliked and distrusted the sex'. This is quite a profound statement and I would say that his behaviour towards certain clients, and indeed Mrs Husdon herself, would suggest that he didn't dislike women at all. I think this was an exaggeration on Watson's part, and as Holmes had no male friends either I think we can say that Holmes disliked and distrusted humankind in general.

I give this story a deserved 9 out of 10.

56 Stories in 56 Days – The Disappearance of Lady Frances Carfax

"Oh I remember this one," says husband, "it's got something to do with a coffin."

Yes, it does involve a coffin and a very clever way to get around needing a death certificate for someone you have tried to murder. It's funny how sometimes we remember the stories by the inanimate objects which they contain – such as a pince-nez, a pencil or a deadly cardboard box. But the interesting point about this story is that Holmes sends Watson abroad alone to make preliminary researches into the disappearance of Mrs Carfax, a lonely middle-aged woman. This does show a high-degree of trust but then he ends up being completely critical of Watson's efforts in his usual abrupt manner – "A very pretty hash you have made of it!"

As usual, Watson simply forgives this rather rude and ungrateful outburst and they carry on together with the investigation. Watson is a very forgiving man and sometimes behaves like a submissive wife. It's one of those stories when you want to reach into the pages, take hold of him and shout – "Come on Watson, man-up!" Poor Watson had told us at the start of the story that he was feeling 'Rheumatic and old' but then landed up feeling like a failure.

Lady Carfax is forty and when I first read this story as a youngster I distinctly remember thinking how old this was. The lady I pictured in my head back then was grey, wrinkled and past her best. Now that I'm in my thirties my whole attitude about the story is different and I picture a glamorous lady travelling around Europe turning heads with her style and sophistication.

I do find the story a little dull until the rather sinister discovery of the unusual coffin. It certainly is a shock when Holmes opens it up to find a genuine dead person in there who died of natural causes. But then, of course, he realises why the coffin was so large for such a small old lady and rushes to stop it leaving for the funeral. This time he forces open the lid and finds two bodies inside, the lifeless old lady and a chloroformed Lady Francis who is moments from suffocation. This is a fantastic twist in the tale, I remember how completely unexpected it was the first time I read it.

Holmes is very active in this one too, bursting into the house without a warrant twice, waving a gun around and shouting the orders – very dramatic. The stories are often full of brawn as well as brains and this one is a fine example.

The disappearance of Lady Frances Carfax scores 8 out of 10.

It's 1897, Holmes is exhausted again and goes off to Cornwall for a rest, but, coincidently, a double murder ends up occurring in the vicinity.

People of Victorian England beware – if Sherlock Holmes comes to stay in your area, trouble won't be far behind him. Holmes must be the unluckiest person in history when it comes to holidays as yet again a break is interrupted by tragedy. But this is certainly a queer one.

With the help of an early start I was able to read the story and make some notes before starting work and intended to type things up on the train while travelling home, as I had other commitments this evening. Well, the train was absolutely packed, people jammed into every corner and no chance of even a seat, let alone a table. I ended up having to sit on the dirty floor with people standing all around me and type with the laptop balanced precariously on my knee. Someone trod on my foot and another thrust their bag in my face – suffice to say I was pretty grumpy but did manage to type this up and load it onto my site at the usual time. Holmes and Watson didn't have to contend with all this on the steam trains of Victorian London did they? And I bet the trains were never late either...

Anyway, back to the story. A local man is apparently devastated and mystified when his sister dies and his two brothers are driven insane by a sudden, unknown horror. Then we have a distant relative from overseas (Yes, I know, yet another culprit from distant shores) who turns up acting very suspiciously. The local man is also murdered mid-investigation prompting Holmes to test out his theory on both himself and poor, loyal Watson.

Holmes suspects that an air-born poison is responsible for what has happened after finding traces of it around a lamp which had been used as a combustion device. Things then take on an unexpected turn when he sits with Watson in a room, lights the lamp and lays the powder upon it. Watson is given the option to back out of this risky experiment but stands fast and Holmes affectionately sates – 'I thought I knew my Watson'. Dangerous mental terror grips them both as poison fills the room and it is Watson, sitting furthest from the lamp, who grabs Holmes, drags him free and out into the fresh air before it is too late.

Whilst lying on the grass, Holmes makes a very heartfelt apology to Watson for what he has just put him through causing Watson to remark that he had never seen so much of Holmes' heart before. What a lovely line, and a reminder that a great heart really does beat behind the reasoned and clinical exterior. In response to this apology, Watson replies – 'It is my greatest joy and privilege to help you.' Gosh, not sure if I could be quite that forgiving myself.

The story contains one of my favourite exchanges:

"I followed you,"

"I saw no one,"

"That is what you may expect to see when I follow you."

There is also a less-famous but very significant line in this tale which I think explains so much about Holmes mental processes – 'To let the brain work without sufficient material is like racing an engine. It racks itself to pieces'.

This is it; this is the truth about Sherlock Holmes to me. He uses work not to stimulate his great brain, but to channel it, control it. Without work his mind races away full of compulsions and overwhelming ideas, a torrent of mental processes. He uses drugs and music not to stimulate but to subdue. And when he has nothing professional to focus on, he has to have something to distract and control this flood of mental activity so conducts intense studies into things like music of the middle-ages or chemical experiments. It's not that he wants to keep his brain active, more that it overwhelms him without an outlet, a pressure-valve.

Holmes admits he has never loved in this story. I have always found this somewhat unrealistic – a man of that age who has never experienced love. But I suppose we have to take it as true considering that he tells us so himself. Or does he have secrets which he wants to keep hidden?

Yet again, Holmes lets the culprit escape justice even though a murder has been committed. He listens to the man's story and decides that his actions were justified.

I'm not terribly taken with the story itself but it certainly is a revealing one, packed full of insight into the character of Sherlock Holmes – therefore I have to give it 8 out of 10.

56 Stories in 56 Days – His Last Bow – An Epilogue of Sherlock Holmes

Well, this one is certainly very different, but then, there was a war on.

Written in the third person, this unusual tale is set during the First World War and sees a sixty-year-old Holmes come out of retirement to trap a brilliant German spy. It takes him two years and involves taking on the persona of a cocky Irish-American with colourful dialogue and a goatee beard.

The story has a very different feel to the ones set in an earlier time. Here we have mention of a 100 horse-power Benz car, the electric light switch, spark plugs, coppers (as in policemen), dough (as in money) and various other Americanisms. The world is changing and I think Conan Doyle wanted his writing to reflect this.

I suppose this is where I have a problem with the story. It seems a bit like Doyle felt he needed to do something war-related and put this together rather hurriedly. Perhaps I am being too harsh but when you pull the plot apart some things just don't make sense.

Holmes has been supplying Von Bork (the spy) with incorrect information for two years, surely someone must have noticed by now that the info is false? And would the German really tell him so freely the pass-code for the safe?

The stereotypes are alive and well too – the sporty German, cocky American and the 'Thickset chauffeur' in the form of a very solid, English, Watson.

There is naturally that hint of propaganda too, the way the German is so dismissive of the English for example. He describes his house-keeper as having 'Complete self-absorption and general air of comfortable somnolence', underestimating her completely as she is actually working for Holmes and part of the plot to trap Von Bork.

English spirit and resolve triumph over German cunning but still the spirit of fair play remains. Holmes doesn't physically hurt the German, much to the relief of the housekeeper who says that despite everything he has been a good master to her. Holmes even offers him a cigar. The Brits are certainly made out to be the gracious heroes in true propaganda style.

The ending is somewhat sad as Holmes and Watson say goodbye, not sure when they will see each other again due to the winds of war blowing across England bringing change and danger, 'A good many of us may wither before its blast.' I am left desperate to know what happens to them next.

7 out of 10.

56 Stories in 56 Days – The Adventure of the Illustrious Client

The best part of this story has to be the fiery and fabulous Miss Kitty Winter. At last, a feisty, strong and determined woman who we can really believe in. Kitty Winter is my favourite minor character in all the stories and she even played her part in inspiring the protagonist in my own novel. She is a raw and honest woman of ill-repute who storms into the lives of Holmes and Watson, brought along by Holmes' underworld agent Shinwell, to help persuade a highly-duped society woman against marrying the evil Baron Gruner. Kitty herself was duped into loving him once and came to know his evil secrets before being tossed aside. She is hungry for revenge and full of spirit – a revenge she ultimately gets in a very dramatic fashion.

Holmes has been commissioned by an illustrious client who is not named (via an agent) to prevent Miss Violet de Merville from marrying the evil Baron. He murdered his first wife and is a prolific philanderer, even keeping a little book with pictures and details of all his conquests. The silly young girl has fallen for all his lies and will not listen to reason. Holmes takes Kitty around to see her in the hope that her testimony will make her see reason but despite the passionate words Kitty delivers, Miss Merville remains steadfast.

Here again we see Holmes resort to burglary to achieve results, as he breaks into the Baron's house to snatch the book while Watson keeps the Baron occupied by pretending to be an expert in Chinese pottery. The Baron spots Holmes and rushes to stop him but Kitty jumps out and throws acid in his face, her perfect act of revenge. The baron's beautiful features which he has used to ensnare many vulnerable women melt before their eyes.

Holmes has got the book and it is passed on to Miss Merville, prompting her to swiftly call off the engagement.

I do love this story; it's silly, fantastical, a bit over-the-top but great fun and a real page turner. It does leave me with unanswered questions though such as – who was the illustrious client? Do we really care anymore when we have become used to Holmes working for royalty and the Prime Minister? Why was the Baron so intent on marrying this woman? It can't have been simply for money as he had plenty of his own. Was it for respectability or was it simply because he could? And why has Watson moved out of 221b to take rooms at Queen Anne Street? Has he re-married?

As this is the first story in The Case Book, we are treated to a preface written by Sir Arthur Conan Doyle. This is a rather strange piece in which he makes it clear that he has had enough of Sherlock Holmes, only brought him back from the dead due to public pressure, and sees the work as somewhat inferior to his other more lofty endeavours such as historical writings, poetry and psychic research. Don't get me wrong, he doesn't exactly come out and state all this but the inferences are clear. For me, this makes for a rather negative start to The Case Book which is a shame as the first story is such an enjoyable one.

For Kitty and wronged women everywhere – The Illustrious Client gets 9 out of 10.

* The late, very great Jeremy Brett would have celebrated his 78th birthday today. He was the man who brought the canon alive to me on screen. We must never forget his compelling and sensitive performances.

For the first time, Holmes takes up Watson's challenge and writes the story himself.

The story is written in the first person and is Holmes' attempt to write up the details of a case himself, rather than have his exploits trumpeted by Watson's words. He does admit to criticising Watson's accounts for being too superficial and sensational rather than just sticking to the facts. Trying to do it himself however, does force Holmes to confess that it is more difficult than he thought and that a degree of superficial information is needed in order to interest the reader. How pleasant it is to hear him make this u-turn and give Watson a little credit for the works which did so much to bring details of his career to a wide audience.

But this pleasing observation is then somewhat ruined by what I have always found to be a rather upsetting and disappointing statement. Holmes sets out to explain his association with Watson and basically tells us that the union is devoid of sentiment on his part and more practical than emotional − 'I would take this opportunity to remark that if I burden myself with a companion in my various little inquiries it is not done out of sentiment or caprice, but it is that Watson has some remarkable characteristics of his own to which in his modesty he has given small attention amid his exaggerated estimates of my own performances'. So, in summary, he didn't really care much for Watson but let him tag along because he was useful – or at least that's how he makes it sound.

I have never really known what to make of this statement. All the evidence contained within the other stories contradicts it and suggests that Holmes cared greatly for Watson in spite of his general disinclination for friendships. So why say it? It's almost as if he is ashamed of spending time with someone out of sentiment and feels the need to justify it with a practical reason.

Also of interest is that Holmes tells us Watson has 'deserted' him for a wife. The year is 1903 so this must be the doctor's second wife, and yet we know absolutely nothing about her. This is one of the many unanswered questions I try to tackle in my own novel and I'd love nothing more than to talk about the how-and-why of it but don't want to spoil the surprise for those yet to read it.

As to the rest of the story of the blanched soldier, it is certainly an imaginative one. A fit and healthy young soldier gets wounded in the Boer war and accidently spends the night in an unmade bed at a leper hospital. He returns home to England and starts to develop white patches on his face. Presuming them to be the mark of leprosy and in fear of him being forever segregated, his parents hide him in an outhouse. A fellow soldier is concerned that he has not heard from his friend and visits his family home to seek him out. The cover story that the young man has gone on a round-the-world voyage is dismissed and he goes to Holmes for help.

All ends well when Holmes uncovers the truth and, very kindly, takes along a specialist who declares that whatever afflicts the boy, it is not leprosy after all.

I do really like the narrative but it is interesting to note that for all his criticism of Watson's writing, Holmes' account runs along in the same sort of formula with all the usual Watson-esque embellishments. And that cold declaration about his lack of sentiment or caprice for Watson does rather spoil things for me.

Only a 7 out of 10 for this one I'm afraid.

56 Stories in 56 Days – The Adventure of the Mazarin Stone

This story really does save the best till last.

Written in the third person and detailing the disappearance of a valuable precious stone, this story gets off to a rather slow start and I miss Watson's narrative voice. Maybe it was because I was reading at 5.30am, but I have to confess that I fell asleep half way through and woke up just in time to rush out of the house and get my train to work. I'm sitting on it now and despite the middle of the story sending me to sleep – the ending was great and got my full attention.

Count Sylvius, a typical upper-class wrong 'un, has stolen the stone and Holmes has all the evidence against him but still doesn't know where the gem has been hidden. Knowing that the Count is pretty keen to see him dead, Holmes sets up a life-like dummy in the window of 221b in the hope that it will be this, and not he, which any bullets are directed towards. He then gets the Count to visit him and offers to let him go as long as he gives up the stone's location.

He calls up the count's associate who is standing guard in the street and allows them time to confer together. He tells them that he will go into another room and play on his violin so as to not hear their conversation but actually uses a secret door to nip in behind the curtain and sit it place of the dummy. A gramophone plays violin music to foil the pair and as Holmes listens to their conversation, the count reveals that he has the stone upon him. Holmes suddenly springs out from hiding, takes the stone and facilitates their arrest. Hurrah!

Then the client is summoned and Holmes can't help having a little more sport. Lord Cantlemere is very sceptical of Holmes abilities and sneers when the detective suggests that he has not been able to find the stone. He actually slips it into the Lord's pocket and happily toys with him before revealing the truth. This is brilliant, great fun and, as always, it is most enjoyable to see Holmes get one over a difficult client or official.

This is also the story in which we meet Billy, the wise young page, who seems to have taken over some of Watson's role and 'Helped a little to fill up the gap of loneliness and isolation which surrounded the saturnine figure of the great detective'.

Watson does seem rather surplus to requirements in this one as his only role is to go for the police. He doesn't even write up the story and therefore a strange air of chance seems to hang over proceedings – Watson is much older now, has a life of his own but Holmes' world has not changed leaving him rather lonely except for his young page.

It's hard for me to score this one as I didn't really think much of it until the concluding moments and though Billy is a spirited young man, he is no match for Watson. I have to give it just 6 out of 10, especially as the dummy idea is hardly new – having featured so heavily in The Empty House.

Mrs Klein is the ultimate cougar, and much more interesting than Irene Adler in my opinion.

Here we return to the familiar narration of Doctor Watson and encounter a ruthless woman who hires a band of ruffians to protect her interests. This story also contains some great minor characters that feature in my own novel – the boxer Steve Dixie and the gossip Langdale Pike. I particularly love Pike, who makes a hearty living out of collecting and passing on society gossip. I would love to have heard more about him throughout the stories and really enjoyed the way Granada presented him in their dramatisation of this story.

The title of this story also features in Barefoot, though not in its entirety. I blended together the names 'Wisteria Lodge' and 'Three Gables' to create Wisteria Gables, the property in my story which becomes almost as significant as 221b.

We have another Birmingham reference in this story too – Steve Dixie says that he has been training at the Bull Ring in Birmingham. What a lovely reminder of what the Bull Ring was before it became a major shopping centre with shiny fittings and a luxury department store. Blimey, times have changed!

The story is simple enough, though Granada did a brilliant job of embellishing it and made it into one of my favourite episodes. Isadora Klein is a great villainess, cunning, beautiful, with a preference for young men and enough money to call the shots.

The story starts with Holmes being threatened by Dixie, which only serves to whet his curiosity and prompt him to investigate the case of a sweet old lady who has had a generous but strange offer made on her property. An agent informs her that his client wishes to purchase not only her house but also all the furniture. The money offered is very generous and enough for her to fulfil an ambition to travel around the world. Only trouble is, she is not allowed to remove anything from the house except a few personal possessions under supervision. At this point, she contacts Holmes for help and the involvement of Dixie, and the gang leader Barney Stockdale, convinces him that the matter is serious.

It turns out that the lady's handsome young son had died recently of a broken heart and his possessions are being stored in the house. He had been seduced and then dumped by the heartless Klein because he was of common birth. As an act of revenge he had written a scandalous novel all about their affair.

As she was about to marry a titled young man, a scandal would threaten this union and that's why she tried to buy the house and everything in it – to get her hands on the manuscript. When this failed a burglary was staged and the writings snatched. Holmes visits her to get it back but it is too late, the papers have been burned. Holmes threatens to unleash the scandal unless she writes out a cheque for enough money to travel around the world. This she eventually does and the sweet old lady gets to fulfil her ambition.

It's another example of Holmes genuinely caring about his client and going above and beyond to help them. Mrs Klein still seems to get off lightly in my opinion though as a scandal is avoided and she probably does manage to ensnare the titled young man who she is clearly using for social advancement only. In the Granada episode Holmes forces her to break off the engagement and her plans are thwarted. I have to say that I do prefer that ending.

A good story with a surprisingly contemporary feel – 7 out of 10.

Well, it's not exactly Buffy or Twilight but it's just as far-fetched.

I really want to like this story – it's something a bit different and the title makes it sound very exciting but I just can't warm to it. I think it's because I don't find the plot very believable. Would you really risk your own marriage and the love of your husband just to protect him from heartbreak over the realities of his eldest son? Would you really take the blame knowing that it might cost you your marriage and threaten the future of your own child? And if you feared that a quiver of arrows might be used to harm your child surely you would remove them, not leave them hanging on the wall? And is it fair to send a disabled young boy, despite his wrongdoings, away to sea for a year?

So many questions and not enough satisfactory answers for my liking I'm afraid. Which is a shame really as the general premise of the story is a good one. Mr Ferguson comes to see Holmes to ask for help in clearing up a very unpleasant incident in his household. He had married a beautiful, spirited South American woman and had no doubt over her love and devotion for him. They had a baby together but he also had a son from a previous marriage who had a spinal condition. He had witnessed his wife beating this youth on two occasions and then found her crouched over the baby with blood around her mouth and a wound on the child's neck. She fled to her bedroom and he hasn't seen her since.

Holmes managed to deduce from the weapons on the wall and a curiously disabled dog that a poisoned arrow had been shot into the child's neck by the jealous eldest boy. The wife, who was anticipating such an attack, was trying to suck the poison out. She hid the truth from her husband as she didn't want to break his heart over the son whom he loved so much.

Like I say at the start, there is so much about this that doesn't quite hold true that it detracts from the story for me. However, it is still a good tale at its heart and I did enjoy re-reading it.

It is also the story in which Holmes says the line – 'I never get your limits Watson. There are unexplored possibilities about you', upon hearing of Watson's earlier prowess on the rugby field. I have used this idea to great effect in my own novel and tried to explore some of those previously unexplored possibilities.

There is also another expression which seemed more like something my Nan would say rather than a wealthy gentleman, a bit like the 'I'll just put my slippers on' line in The Blue Carbuncle. Mr Ferguson says – 'And yet the kiddies have got to be protected.' Kiddies? I can hear my mum's voice in my head saying "Kids are baby goats not human children!" – her usual phrase of chastisement if I ever said 'kid' instead of child.

A disappointing story overall but still gives the usual enjoyment of watching Holmes save the day. 6 out of 10.

Ah yes, it's the one where Watson gets shot.

The story begins with Watson telling us that Holmes has refused a knighthood for services which he could not describe at that particular time. This fits in well with Holmes' lack of ambition beyond solving problems which others cannot. He is so much more likable and complex as a result. The complexity comes from being both unpretentious but also adoring praise all at the same time. A spontaneous round of applause from Watson and a group of constables means more to him than a knighthood.

Watson goes on to describe his position as that of 'Partner and confidant' which is quite a statement really. As I have remarked before, the use of the word 'partner' infers an equal footing to Holmes and a dependency upon each other which acknowledges the contributions of both to the success of the, shall we say, detective agency.

This story has similarities to The Red-Headed League, in that it's about someone finding an ingenious method of getting a person out of the way. An elaborate ruse is concocted with the sole purpose of getting an eccentric old collector to leave his house so that someone can break in and plunder the forger's den set up in his cellar by the previous occupant. The collector is called Nathan Garrideb and is so absorbed by his collection of curios that he rarely ever leaves the house. The American villain (yes it's another foreign baddie) who wants access to the house has to invent a tale to shift him, and uses his unusual name as a starting point.

Pretending to be a Mr John Garrideb, the American claims that he has been left a fortune by an eccentric millionaire whose name was also Garrideb. He can only claim the money if he can find two other men with the same surname, then they will receive a third each. He claims to have come recently to London (a lie which Holmes dismisses due to his English outfit being clearly well-worn) upon hearing that a Garrideb resided there. He then tells Nathan Garrideb that the third man has been found and that he must go and meet with him in order to seal the deal.

Eager to inherit the money and add rare artefacts to his collection, Mr Nathan agrees to leave his house and go. Fortunately, Holmes has deduced the real reason for his departure and lies in wait with Watson to catch the American. This is where things take on a dramatic turn and Watson pays the price for following Holmes into danger.

Upon realising that he has been caught out, the American turns his weapon on poor Watson and shoots him in the thigh. And here we see the strongest evidence of Holmes' genuine depth of emotion for his friend. Holmes smashes his pistol down on the man's head then rushes to put his arms around his friend, helping him to a chair and asking most earnestly – "You are not hurt Watson? For God's sake, say that you are not hurt!"

These two sentences are full of concern, a touch of panic and perhaps even a little guilt knowing that he put his friend in harm's way. But it is what Watson tells us which is the most poignant of all – 'It was worth a wound-it was worth many wounds-to know the depth of loyalty and love which lay behind that cold mask. The clear, hard eyes were dimmed for a moment, and the firm lips were shaking. For the one and only time I caught a glimpse of a great heart as well as of a great brain. All my years of humble but single-minded service culminated in that moment of revelation.'

What a fantastic and profound statement to make. This shows as much about Watson's love for Holmes as vice-versa. So there we have it, Holmes was without doubt capable of great emotion and did truly love his friend despite often being cold and difficult. And Watson clearly longed for that love – or for the confirmation of it at least.

After tearing Watson's trousers with his pocket-knife and discovering to much relief that the wound is superficial, Holmes turns on the American and says – "By the Lord, it is as well for you. If you had killed Watson, you would not have got out of this room alive." And I really think he meant it.

I really enjoyed this story on two levels. Firstly for the narrative itself – this is very clever, albeit far-fetched, and certainly makes you want to turn the page to see how it all ends up. And secondly, for the insight it gives into the relationship between these two men and their enduring friendship. Here we see an emotional Holmes, the emotion we always knew him capable of but had never seen to this extent before.

I have to give this a 9 out of 10

The contents of that despatch-box at Cox and Co bank sound like something out of the X-Files.

Watson begins this story by telling us about his despatch-box hidden in the vaults of Cox and Co bank crammed full of records of curious cases. They seem to be of a mysterious nature, almost supernatural – perhaps linking in with Doyle's growing interest in spiritualism. We hear of Mr James Phillimore who goes back into his house for an umbrella and disappears, the ship which sails into a patch of mist from which it never emerges, and poor Mr Persano who was found 'Stark-staring mad with a matchbox in front of him which contained a remarkable worm, said to be unknown to science'. Enough there to keep Mulder and Scully busy for some time.

This particular story is of a more worldly nature and involves the usual formula of a passionate and fiery foreign woman, a Brazilian in fact, and a ruthless rich American. According to Doyle, most of our country estates seemed to have been owned by people, English or otherwise, who had made their fortunes abroad and thought, "Oh, do you know what would be nice? Retiring to the British countryside and buying up a big old country pile. Then we will do some wrong-doing to keep ourselves occupied."

In this case, the American bullies his wife and staff. The poor wife has lost the love of her husband, as well as her looks, and now has to watch him fawning all over the pretty young governess who has captured his heart. She contrives to kill herself and ensure that her rival is blamed for the crime. She ties a heavy stone to a revolver and dangles this over the bridge so that it will be pulled into the water the instant she pulls the trigger. An identical gun with a cartridge missing has already been hidden in the young woman's wardrobe. A note in the governess's handwriting arranging to meet on the bridge further compounds the case against her and all is set for the vengeful wife to get exactly the result she wanted. But as with the Boscombe Valley Mystery, which I always confuse with this story for some reason, Holmes is able to save an innocent person despite all the evidence against them.

I really enjoyed re-visiting this story and the outcome is one of the best twists to any of the short stories. Things are very well set up to make you think that the husband is guilty or perhaps the governess did it in some form of self defence. The actual truth is quite a revelation.

Holmes is on great form noticing the mark in the stonework of the bridge which turns out to be the key to the whole mystery. Observation at its best and the science of deduction clearly at work. A well-deserved 9 out of 10.

Love can make us do stupid things and that is certainly true in the case of poor old Professor Presbury.

This is one of the most unbelievable of all the stories in my opinion but I do rather like it all the same. The poor old professor has fallen madly in love with a young girl and starts taking a dangerous elixir which is meant to restore his youth.

Instead, it makes him creep around dragging his knuckles along the floor and climb up walls like a monkey. The potion contains extracts from a Himalayan climbing monkey which is what caused his alarming symptoms.

The story is so fantastical yet somehow, as you read it, you do find yourself believing every word and getting completely drawn-in. It's memorable too, unlike many of the stories which are so similar to others and formulaic that it is difficult to separate them in your memory. And with the modern boom in rejuvenating procedures such as Botox, face-lifts, Liposuction, fillers, and even a recent discovery of injecting sheep extracts into the face to plump it up, perhaps there was something rather prophetic about Doyle's idea.

Thinking about it, it doesn't actually seem very fantastical at all compared to modern ideas – but I do think a monkey elixir would have caused far more serious, possibly fatal, effects - not just a bit of moodiness, creeping and climbing.

143

We are told by Watson that this is one of Holmes' last cases before retirement. This is sad really, being reminded that it all comes to an end and, like with us all, Holmes must grow old. Watson also gives a description of the state of their friendship at that time. He has become an institution, a habit, like the violin and shag tobacco. The relations between the two men are described as 'Peculiar' due to their strangely utilitarian nature. It is, as always, a friendship, but Watson is a friend-with-benefits (though not in *that way* of course). Watson is a 'Whetstone for his mind' and a comrade, 'Upon whose nerve he could place some reliance'. Friendship is tinged with usefulness, and a comfortable, familiarity now characterises their relationship.

They can each be themselves and appreciate these traits, these points of difference, in one another. Indeed, Holmes summons Watson with a message saying – 'Come at once if convenient-if inconvenient come all the same.' Is this disrespectful or just being yourself? Is it Holmes exercising his superiority or acknowledging how much he needs his friend's help? This is the problem with trying to analyse Holmes, that duality at the core of his personality shifting between kindness and emotion, then coldness and arrogance.

A great story with interesting observations from Watson about the autumn days of their friendship. 8 out of 10.

In my memory, this was one of my favourites but reading it again today I can't entirely understand why.

I approached this story full of excitement because, though I haven't read it for some years I remember really enjoying it first time around. I think it was the descriptions of the location which I particularly enjoyed – the little cottage on the South Downs with a view across the channel, the coastline of chalk cliffs, the little path down to the beach, and the beach itself with its hollows and curves making perfect swimming pools. Doesn't it sound idyllic? Perfect, beautiful, coastal England sunlit and shimmering in your mind's eye.

But the location is not enough to fill the gap left behind by Watson who is completely absent from this story. Holmes makes another attempt at being his own chronicler and tells us that, 'At this period of my life the good Watson had passed almost beyond my ken. An occasional weekend visit was the most that I ever saw of him.'

This seems so sad really, though rather inevitable. Watson is, after all, a normal man who has friends, a job, possibly a family by now. Naturally he would not give all this up to spend his time pottering around the Downs bothering Holmes in his retirement and waiting to be summoned by the great man to help out with bee-keeping and the odd disappearing local. But somehow, things just aren't the same without him and it does seem sad to think of Holmes all alone without any real friends except Mr Stackhurst who was, 'The only man who was on such terms with me that we could drop in on each other in the evenings without an invitation.' Hardly the same as the intimacy he shared with Watson for all those years.

I do still like this story and did enjoy re-reading it. I remember that it was the only Holmes story where I actually worked out whodunit before Holmes did when I read it for the first time. No wonder I enjoyed it so much. I didn't get quite as far as knowing it was a jelly-fish who had caused the poor man his agonizing death but did work out that it must have been a sea creature of some-sort. Even reading it again today I still think that Holmes was very slow to come to his conclusions, which he does admit himself. Perhaps it's old-age getting the better of him.

We learn that Holmes lives near to a coaching establishment where young men go to study and prepare for various professions. One of the professors, McPherson, enjoys taking a morning swim in the perfect natural pools, as does Holmes himself who often joins him. This does seem like a surprisingly social thing for him to do and perhaps he is not quite as friendless as he first makes out. However, poor McPherson goes out for a swim as usual but gets stung all over his back and shoulders by the tentacles of a deadly jelly-fish called the Lion's Mane.

Holmes and Stackhurst find him on lying on the cliff path, obviously dying and covered in horrible bleeding lacerations. He manages to whisper the words "Lion's mane," before finally giving up his struggle. It looks to Holmes and his companion that the man has been flogged to death and murder is suspected. Various false avenues of investigation are then pursued until Holmes finally hits upon the truth.

The investigation doesn't involve a huge amount of detective work and the story doesn't contain many examples of Holmes' incredible powers of observation and analysis, even though he does ultimately solve the case.

Holmes tells us an interesting piece of information in this story about his attitude towards woman – 'Women have seldom been an attraction to me, for my brain has always governed my heart.'' Seldom is certainly not never, and I do take this to mean that Holmes has been attracted to women and has on rare occasions indulged in his feelings but that ultimately his brain has quashed the longings of his heart. This is a much more realistic interpretation in my opinion than to say Holmes has never had any experiences with women at all.

All in all, it's a good story with a beautiful setting and a little food-for-thought about Holmes and Watson, their changing relationship in later years and this startling use of the word 'seldom' which I take to be a confession of occasional attraction to the opposite sex. It has to score 8 out of 10.

56 Stories in 56 Days – The Adventure of the Veiled Lodger

Here we have another mysterious lodger with a past to hide, but this story is very different to The Red Circle even though I do keep getting them confused.

This is a common problem for me, getting the stories mixed-up because of the similarities between them. So many include women with violent husbands, dodgy deeds committed abroad, foreign baddies with an axe to grind, old lovers reappearing, governesses in trouble – I mean, surely I'm not the only one who confuses the Copper Beeches with the Solitary Cyclist? But then, in fairness to Doyle, it would be almost impossible to come up with 56 stories without touching on common themes across the series. Love, loss, the past catching up with someone, occur over and over again in most works of literature including my own – I am certainly not saying all this as a criticism, more as an explanation of why the stories can blur and merge sometimes in my mind.

Anyway, onto this particular story and there really isn't much to say. It's another one of those which can be described as a good story but not necessarily a good Holmes story. The tale itself is fine, but Holmes has very little to do with it. He gets called in because the woman, the veiled lodger, needs someone to listen to her story before she takes her own life. That's all Holmes is, just an ear. He doesn't have to investigate anything, use his fantastic powers of observation or analyse at the scene.

He just listens then shows a surprising level of sympathy and compassion and persuades the woman not to take her own life. Okay, so he does technically save a life, but not much else really.

The woman was married to a violent lion-tamer and has an affair with the circus' strong man. They devise a plan to kill the husband but it back-fires and she gets horribly injured by the lion, condemning her to a lonely life of isolation, hidden behind a veil to conceal her terrible scars. She has never told anyone about the crime as her husband's death was put down as being caused by a lion attack. This plays on her conscience and prompts her landlady to suggest she unburden herself to Holmes.

And that's it really, wish there was more to add but I don't feel this story moves us forward in our understanding of Holmes or is anything other than a mildly diverting short story.

I can only give it 5 out of 10 I'm afraid.

56 Stories in 56 Days – The Adventure of Shoscombe Old Place

This is a great little tale, dark and gothic.

In this story we have crypts, dead bodies, the burning of bones in a furnace, rumours of ghosts - it's all great fun and a wonderful macabre story. There's even a bit of horse racing thrown in which made my husband sit up and pay attention (as I have mentioned before, he is an ex-racing journalist).

This story is such a good example of what a great story-teller Doyle was – not just clever and responsible for creating one of the best-loved characters in English fiction, but really good at spinning an imaginative yarn which is entertaining and a real page-turner.

This is the dilemma isn't it for so many writers? Do you create a work of great intellectual significance which might change the world? Do you use your writing as a vehicle to show-off your intellectual prowess, or do you just try to create an entertaining page-turner that people can't put down? With my book, I went for the latter and aimed for something in-between low-brow and high-brow, an entertaining middle-ground with a mix of literary clout and fast-paced story-telling. I think Doyle made the same choice with Holmes, a choice which he perhaps came to regret when he struggled to get his more serious work recognised – though not when counting his money of course!

The story begins with Holmes bent over a microscope analysing threads from a coat and finding traces of glue amongst the fibres of fabric. He also tells Watson about bringing a coiner to justice by finding the zinc and copper filings in the seam of his cuff. In this way Holmes was such a pioneer – using the science of deduction and forensic analysis rather than old-fashion methods of following a hunch to find the bad guys.

Watson reveals his love of betting on the horses when Holmes asks if he knows anything of the sport – "I ought to. I pay for it with about half my wound pension." Here again we see how Watson is rather carefree when it comes to money, just as with previous examples of him getting Holmes to keep his cheque book and the general lack of business acumen shown towards his medical practice. This side of Watson gave me great creative opportunities in my own novel and I have used his human deficiencies to their full potential.

The story itself is all about Sir Robert Norberton from the estate of Shoscombe Old Place and his money troubles. The estate is actually owned by his sister who inherited it on the death of her husband. He is in debt and has bet all he has on his horse, Shoscombe Prince, to win the Derby. His sister dies of natural causes a week before the race and Sir Robert is so afraid that creditors will descend upon him and claim the horse, that he conceals the death in the hope of stalling things until after the race. He hides her body in a used coffin in the family crypt and burns the bones of the original occupant in a furnace.

Despite his questionable actions, all ends well when Shoscombe Prince wins the Derby and Sir Robert is able to settle his depts. For once, Doyle doesn't really come down on one side or the other with regard to how wrong the protagonist has been and leaves it up to the reader to decide whether the happy ending is deserved or not. For me, I think it ties things up neatly and rounds off an excellent story which shows Holmes and his methods in all their glory. A well deserved 9 out of 10.

56 Stories in 56 Days – The Adventure of the Retired Colourman

Well, that's it, I've made it to the end. This is the 56th story and signals the end of my epic blog-a-thon. What an adventure it has been! Re-visiting the stories has been very enjoyable and being able to share my thoughts on them with people all around the world has remained an exhilarating experience. For all those of you who have stuck with me since the start, a massive "thank you" from me. In a strange way, I shall miss doing this every day. On the other hand, I won't miss getting up at 5.30am to start reading and writing before setting off for work.

Anyway, my journey ends with this fun little story about a miserly old man who murders his attractive young wife and her lover then tries to make it look like they have robbed him and run away. He traps them in an air-tight room and gasses them to death, then starts painting the house to disguise the smell and ditches the bodies down a well. Okay, doesn't exactly sound like a 'fun' story I admit, but Doyle has a way of telling things like this which make them seem more like a dark comedy than a disturbing thriller. Things are played to extremes and this stops the story from being too real, too serious. As I have said before, there is much humour in the short stories for which I don't think Doyle gets enough credit.

Am I the only one who thought a colourman was someone military? For those of you who might have made the same mistake, a colourman is someone who manufactures artistic materials such as paint-boxes.

The story begins with Holmes in a melancholy mood; "But is not all life pathetic and futile? Is not his story a microcosm of the whole? We reach, we grasp. And what is left in our hands at the end? A shadow. Or worse than a shadow-misery." Blimey, someone got out of bed the wrong side.

The colourman is so confident that he will get away with his crimes that he enlists Holmes to track down his wife and lover, even though he took their lives himself. Holmes is too busy to investigate at first and sends Watson in his place. As with Watson's efforts in the search for Lady Carfax, Holmes is very dismissive of his findings – "It is true that in your mission you have missed everything of importance," but this time he does throw in lots of positive comments too. However, Watson's rather poetic and detailed description of the wall around the colourman's house is cut short with a bad tempered remark – "Cut out the poetry Watson," followed by, "I note that it was a high brick wall." Poor Watson, he really is the most patient of men.

My modern-day mind couldn't help but laugh (out loud on the train – rather embarrassing) when Holmes suggests that Watson could have used his natural charms to entice information from local women and adds – "I can picture you whispering soft nothings with the young lady at the Blue Anchor, and receiving hard somethings in exchange." Brilliant, priceless dialogue – possibly even funnier than the classic, "I'll just go and put my slippers on", line in the Blue Carbuncle.

The police inspector working on the case, Mackinnon, does make the point to Holmes that he is able to get results in part because he can get away with doing things which the officials can't. The point has been made before and is very true. Even though Holmes is undeniably brilliant and his fantastic mind is what ultimately brings about the resolutions, being able to break into people's houses, wearing disguises, duping people into leaving their homes unattended, getting engaged to the villain's maid etc are certainly a massive part of his armoury.

In this story, Holmes yet again breaks into a house in order to solve the case. We forgive him, of course, because the ends always justify the means but these tactics are beyond the reach of the official police. But then, they cannot complain as Holmes is always happy to step aside and let them take all the credit. At the end of this story Watson reads out a newspaper article praising MacKinnon for his 'Bold deduction' and lists points which Holmes actually hit on, not the inspector. Mackinnon takes the praise and glory but Holmes has the satisfaction of knowing that, as always, he has succeeded where others failed, bringing light into the darkness.

What a fine example to end on, a story that contains all I love about Holmes. The brilliant observation and deduction, the interplay with Watson, the humour and darkness skilfully blended together by a writer who I have always felt has not achieved the credit deserved in the history of English literature. Commercial success yes, one of the best loved characters ever written yes, but recognition as a literary great akin to Dickens at al – no. Even Doyle's former home, Undershaw, is under threat because the powers-that-be don't see fit to preserve it.

Well, this little mission of mine has reminded me of not only what a great character Holmes was but also taught me to appreciate the stories as a whole and how beautifully crafted they were. I certainly will miss talking about them every day.

I give the Retired Colourman 9 out of 10. That's a positive score to be ending on, and so my friends, goodbye for now but I will be back summarising my scores and some other stats regarding which stories attracted the most views etc. So not really "goodbye", more of a "until next time…"

56 Stories in 56 Days – My Top Scoring Sherlock Holmes Short Stories and Why

Now that the dust has settled after my blogging adventure, I thought it was time to go through my results and start making some analysis of my findings – starting with a list of which stories gained the highest marks:

Charles Augustus Milverton 10

Six Napoleons 10

Silver Blaze 9

Musgrave Ritual 9

Norwood Builder 9

Dancing Men 9

Bruce Partington Plans 9

Dying Detective 9

Illustrious Client 9

Three Garridebs 9

Thor Bridge 9

Shoscombe Old Place 9

Retired Colourman 9

So is there a pattern here? Is there something which these particular stories have in common that ensured their high score or is it just coincidence that they appear in this list together?

I clearly enjoy the stories where Holmes uses his extraordinary powers of observation and deduction to bring light into darkness, to solve that which seems initially unfathomable but once unraveled is simple and clear.

I like to see the science of deduction at work; this is what makes Holmes so different to other fictional detectives. It's the innate way that he can look at something and make a split-second series of connections which would never even occur to anyone else. Like in Silver Blaze when he asks if any of the sheep have been lame recently and upon hearing that they have, is able to confirm his theory that Straker had tried to make Silver Blaze lame with a special knife. He knew that he would have had to practice on another animal first.

All these stories contain moments like this – classic Holmes full of energy rushing around with his magnifying glass or breaking into houses to observe the smallest but most crucial of details. I like to see Holmes being brilliant, almost super-human, I like being able to witness that great but complex brain frantically hunting down a solution in the most workman-like fashion. Deciphering the code in the Dancing Men, following the steps in the Musgrave Ritual, analyzing the mark in the stonework at Thor Bridge, the smell of the paint in the Retired Colourman and playing his part so convincingly in the Dying Detective – all the things I love most about this fascinating character and the workings of his mind.

I also enjoy the stories which reveal details about the closeness of the central friendship between Holmes and Watson – I like to see Holmes show his heart. The main examples of this are contained within these stories – the line 'If you love me' in the Dying Detective, the overwhelming concern for Watson's welfare when in danger as shown in the Three Garridebs (when he is shot) and the Dying Detective (when he lifts the box with the poisoned spike).

I enjoy the stories which contain humour too, often at the expense of a difficult client or the police. This is evident in Silver Blaze (toying with a sceptical Colonel Ross), Six Napoleons (where the police fixate on completely the wrong line of inquiry) and the joyous out-witting of the murderous Retired Colourman.

The story also has to work well in its own right, it has to be a great Holmes story *and* have a brilliant plot to score a top mark. Some of the tales are only one or the other – a great little story but not much Holmesian action (The Veiled Lodger for example) or vice-versa. I think my top stories work on both levels and combine fascinating detection work with a cracking, well-written plot.

When all these ingredients combine, you get a perfect Sherlock Holmes short story. I suppose the only one on my list which doesn't perfectly fit this pattern is Milverton. Holmes doesn't do a huge amount of detection work, nor does he shine light into darkness but Milverton is such a fantastic villain that this makes up for the lack of these elements.

In summary, I clearly enjoyed reading about Holmes at his energetic, twinkly-eyed best, charging around making brilliant observations, breaking into houses, outwitting criminals and police alike, showing his heart as well as his brain, saving the day and raising the occasional smile too. Phew, I don't ask for much do I?

56 Stories in 56 Days – My Least Favourite Sherlock Holmes Short Stories and Why

Well, as my last blog contained details of the stories which came out with the highest scores, it seems only fair to now look at those which scored the least out of ten.

A Scandal in Bohemia – 5

The Five Orange Pips – 5

Gloria Scott – 5

Naval Treaty – 5

Wisteria Lodge – 4

Veiled Lodger – 5

I have made my thoughts on Scandal quite clear in previous blogs so it was no surprise that it appeared on this list. I think there is too much hype about the relationship between Holmes and Irene Adler, and indeed about Miss Adler herself. She didn't exactly outwit Holmes in a clever and spectacular fashion, she simply realised what he was trying to do, took the incriminating photo and ran away. Hardly a fascinating game of cat-and-mouse in my opinion. And as for romantic love, the fact that she happily marries someone else suggests that she did not fall in love with Holmes. Watson makes it clear that Holmes did not have sentimental feelings towards her either. Therefore, all you are left with is a simple story in which Holmes doesn't really solve anything.

I think this sums up pretty well what the issue is with certain stories for me - I like to see Holmes solve things, save the day. In the Orange Pips, all Holmes' deductions come to nothing because he doesn't save young Openshaw's life and though he cleverly identifies the culprits he is unable to bring them to justice because their ship sinks and they die at sea. It is the same in the Gloria Scott, old Mr Trevor dies needlessly and the truth about his past comes out in a letter – not due to anything which Holmes does. In the Veiled Lodger Holmes simply lends his ear to a distressed woman who wants to make a confession. No deduction or solving a difficult crime, no bringing light into darkness – just listening to a sad tale of past woes.

So what about the Naval Treaty, I hear you ask? Yes, I admit that it doesn't exactly fit the pattern and Holmes does solve the case, but it's just too long and complicated for something which is meant to be a short story – in my opinion at least. Same with Wisteria Lodge – this story is so complicated that it has to be split into two parts, and also seems too far-fetched. I like to be able to believe in the story and prefer the simpler, more small-scale adventures. The back-story given in the Gloria Scott is also difficult to believe in.

So, in summary, I don't like it when the short stories act like complicated novels, the heroine acts like something she's not, Holmes fails to save the day and the truth comes out all by itself. Well, when I say 'don't like', what I mean is 'like less' than other Holmes stories which give more satisfying examples of Holmes' abilities, as well as insight into his character and relationship with Watson. I 'like' all the stories, just some a lot more than others.

56 Sherlock Holmes Stories in 56 Days – The Most Viewed Stories

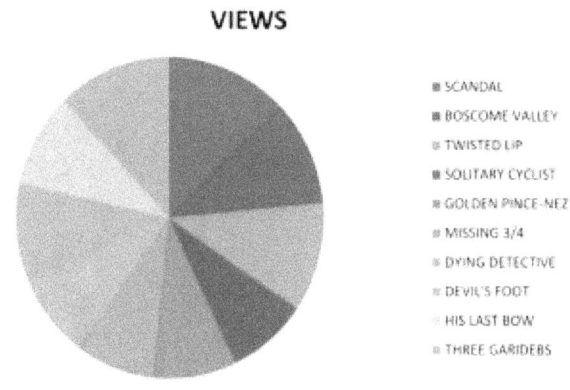

VIEWS

- SCANDAL
- BOSCOME VALLEY
- TWISTED LIP
- SOLITARY CYCLIST
- GOLDEN PINCE-NEZ
- MISSING 3/4
- DYING DETECTIVE
- DEVIL'S FOOT
- HIS LAST BOW
- THREE GARIDEBS

I thought it would be interesting to take a look at which stories attracted the most views during my '56 Stories in 56 Days' series. This has thrown up some unexpected results.

What I expected to find was that the 'big' stories such as The Final Problem and The Empty House would score the highest (neither in fact featured in the top 10) but the most popular was actually A Scandal in Bohemia. Scandal got 13% of the total views out of the top ten most popular stories.

The complete list of the top ten most viewed stories is as follows:

Scandal 13%
Three Garidebs 12%

Boscombe Valley 11%

Twisted Lip – 11%

Devil's Foot – 10%

Golden Pince-Nez – 9%

His Last Bow – 9%

Solitary Cyclist – 8%

Missing Three-Quarter – 8%

Dying Detective – 8%

What is it about Scandal that makes it so fascinating? Whenever I blog about this story, it always attracts a high number of hits. The words 'Irene Adler' are also by far and away the most searched for terms that people have used to find the blog. Readers clearly divide into two distinct camps – those who think Holmes loved Adler, and those who think it's a load of hype over nothing. Perhaps that's what people enjoy about it so much – the debate, the 'what ifs'.

So why did blogs about the other stories on this list attract more traffic than the others?

Well, this list does contain key examples where Holmes reveals the strength of his feelings towards Watson – we get to see his heart as well as his great brain in action. How interesting that Three Garridebs should be second – the story in which Watson gets shot in the leg and Holmes frantically rushes to his aid.

Again in The Devil's Foot we see Holmes full of remorse for testing his theory out on his loyal friend by encouraging him to inhale poison. And, of course, the Dying Detective also reveals the panic Holmes feels when Watson is in danger.

Were people keen to read my interpretation of this interaction in my review? Is that the real truth about Holmes – somehow the criminal aspects of the stories become secondary to the workings of the central friendship and what this reveals about such a complex and fascinating man?

The relationship between the two men is very interdependent – Holmes wouldn't be anywhere near so intriguing if not for his association with his loyal biographer. Picking apart this union and analysing what it reveals about them is a fascination at the heart of the stories for Holmes fans and scholars alike.

And now some thoughts on the long stories, starting with 'A Study in Scarlet'

This feels a bit like the enormity of writing about the Final Problem or The Empty House – can I do justice to such a significant story?

And why is it so significant? Well, simply because it is the first Sherlock Holmes story Conan Doyle wrote. This was where it all began.

Sitting there in his Doctor's surgery between patients, Doyle brought to life a character who went on to become one of the most famous fictional characters of all time. He was 27 years old and wrote this first story in just three weeks. Blimey – it took me seven years to complete my novel, where did I go wrong?

A Study in Scarlet was published in 1887 as part of the Beeton's Christmas Annual, after many rejections. The initial public response was pretty tepid and Holmes didn't capture reader imagination until further works began to appear.

The story begins in 1881, narrated by a young army doctor recently returned from service in Afghanistan. Wounded and lonely he finds himself in London and in need of someone to share rooms with. A chance meeting with an old acquaintance, the never-to-be-seen again Stamford, brings forth an introduction to a young man in a similar predicament who Stamford knows from the laboratory at St Barts hospital. This man is, of course,

Sherlock Holmes, and so begins the legendary partnership which still inspires interest across the globe today.

In this story, Conan Doyle sets up all the elements which come to be as familiar to the Sherlockian as water to ducks.

Doyle is setting out his stall and laying the foundations for the stories yet to come. We learn about the science of deduction and how this makes Holmes different. This is a new kind of detective, scientific and clinical, way ahead of his time. We learn how Watson becomes drawn in to Holmes' work and becomes his biographer, setting up the interdependency at the heart of their relationship. Holmes has all his contrasts out on display – managing to be grumpy, lazy, energetic and playful all in the space of one adventure. We meet Gregson and Lestrade who clearly need Holmes' help but are sceptical and defensive – and ultimately happy to take the credit for his results. Watson is simply enthralled, totally in awe of his new house-mate.

As if all this wasn't enough, we get a story too – a tale full of love, revenge, wrong-doings in foreign lands, oh and the Mormons (who aren't painted in a very good light). And not forgetting the Baker Street Irregulars who also make their debut appearance.

So, did I enjoy re-reading this pivotal story? Well, yes I did, very much, more than I thought I would. I remembered feeling disappointed the first time I read it because a large chunk of the narrative happens in Utah and contains nothing of Holmes and Watson. But reading it back now, I found that I really enjoyed the brilliantly written tale of father and adopted daughter striving to make their way on the plains of Utah. I think it is a mistake when Holmes fans only take interest in the bits which contain their heroes – the stories as a whole are so well written that it is a shame to skip these parts just to get to more Holmes and Watson. In my own novel, Holmes doesn't feature until a few chapters in. I think he is more interesting when viewed as part of a bigger context and in A Study in Scarlet Doyle gets the context just right.

It has to be a 9 out of 10.

The Sign of Four

Sir Arthur Conan Doyle was commissioned to write this story over dinner at the Langham hotel with the managing editor of Lippincott's Monthly Magazine in 1889. The story eventually appeared in the February edition of the magazine in 1890, titled The Sign of the Four. As in A Study in Scarlet, this second Sherlock Holmes story failed to significantly capture the public imagination but did go on to be re-published in several journals and as a book in the same year.

The story begins with Watson informing us about Holmes' drug use, the now infamous seven per-cent solution of cocaine which he has been taking three times a day – wow, I'm no expert but that seems like an awful lot to me. He justifies this by explaining that he finds it 'stimulating and clarifying' because his mind 'rebels at stagnation'. As I have mentioned before, I would argue that the drug use was more about calming that rebellious mind than stimulating it. If your mind is racing around tearing itself to pieces during quiet times, surely you would want to slow it down not the reverse?

Early on in the story we get a description of what exactly a consulting detective is, and how this makes Holmes so different to other private detectives. It's the fact that the police, not just private clients, go to him for help - openly acknowledging that he can solve things which have them baffled. This and Holmes' scientific method of deduction are the two main points at the heart of understanding Holmes and this story re-enforces them well.

The relationship between Holmes and Watson is elaborated on from A Study in Scarlet, taking things further with the description of how Watson wrote up The Study and Holmes criticised it – Watson moves further into the role of helper and biographer rather than simply flat-mate.

We hear more about Holmes' character traits, his moodiness, egotism, how vain he is and that all-important fastidious, focused attention to detail. We learn of his monographs on tobacco and footprints and his ability to tell someone's trade from just their hands. He knows Watson has been to the post office just by observing the mud on his shoes and does a pretty thorough job of analysing Watson's pocket watch – rattling out painful family secrets to the poor man in his characteristic cold and clinical manner. In this story, I think some of the best deductions happen before the case even starts. Holmes analysing Watson is far more entertaining than him turning his powers on the general public.

Now Watson's wound from his military service has mysteriously changed from his shoulder to his leg. I guess Conan Doyle was a very busy man, what with being a doctor and knocking out great books at the same time, so we can forgive him the odd mistake.

Things I really love about this story – the romance between Watson and Mary Morstan (so delightfully sweet and old-fashioned), Toby the dog (great bit of light-relief), Thaddeus Sholto (like a character out of Lewis Carroll), the mysterious pearl which Mary receives every year and the fact that Athelney Jones initially arrests just about everyone except the right person (hilarious – love it when the police get it so wrong but think they are so very right).

Things I don't like – well, the rest of the plot really. At the risk of sounding like a bit of a whinge-bag, I just find it all too complicated and far-fetched. In fact, despite having just finished reading it, if you were to ask me exactly what happened I would struggle to explain. There's basically the Agra treasure, from the city of Agra in India, stolen by a man working at the Fort and his two fellow guards (there's a fourth one too who isn't around for some reason but this is where the title 'Sign of Four comes from). They are arrested for murder, separated from each other, can't go back for the treasure as planned and then (due to a very long, convoluted set of circumstances) someone else gets hold of it and brings it to England. Mary's father has a claim on it but is murdered when he tries to stake his claim. His son feels that Mary is a wronged woman and therefore sends her a pearl each year. That's the gist of it – sort of!

It's all pretty much okay until they capture the culprit and then we get his long, complicated account of the back-story behind the crimes. Maybe I'm just being a bit harsh but I found this difficult to follow and even harder to believe in. Very imaginative though, Conan Doyle certainly knew how to spin out a tale.

On a final note, the Irregulars make another appearance in this story and I play out almost exactly the same scene in Barefoot on Baker Street, just adding in my own protagonist. Even the time of day is the same, the breakfast of ham and eggs and much of the dialogue. This again demonstrates what I was trying to achieve, weave the original stories into a completely new narrative but leave them as intact as possible. And even though I do say it myself, I really like the idea that the first time my central character meets Holmes she is one of the Irregulars – blowing my own trumpet? No, surely not...

Can only give this one 6 out of 10 – mainly for a cute dog and even cuter old fashioned romance. Oh and some great detection at the start, just a shame it gets overtaken by such a complicated back-story.

The Hound of the Baskervilles

Arguably the most well-known of all the stories, long or short, The Hound has become a bit of a legend all of its own. And, it holds the honour of being the first Sherlock Holmes story I ever read – bought from a second-hand book stall for about 20p when I was a child. I started to read it and my mind flooded with images of the fearful, foggy moors, the horrors of the pony dying in the great Grimpen Mire, the dreadful hell-hound with his fangs and flames, the evil Stapleton, the escaped convict, the abused wife and dashing baronet – what's not to love? I was quickly hooked and totally fascinated by the mind and character of the man upon whom the whole narrative hung – Sherlock Holmes.

I was a bit of an eccentric child, given to fantasy, bit of a loner (except for a few much loved friends) and given to striding off on strange adventures. I didn't follow the pack or try to be fashionable, popular, or for want of a better word – normal. So in Holmes I recognised a fellow eccentric and loved him for it – somehow it felt as if he legitimised me, made being different cool. A life-long enjoyment was born and I will always regard The Hound with great affection for that reason.

The story first appeared in The Strand magazine in serialisation form between August 1901 to April 1902 – that's a long time to wait and see whodunit. Holmes had been 'killed off' by his creator in 1893 in The Final Problem but after a break of eight years, Sir Arthur decided to write this new story which pre-dated that fateful tale. He was inspired by the story of Squire Richard Cabell – an evil Devonshire man who, after his death allegedly lead a pack of ghostly hounds across the moors. Interestingly, Doyle did know a Baskerville family and even stayed with them at Baskerville Hall, but it was located in Wales rather than Devon. Doyle changed the location to protect his friends from the intrusion of tourists.

Unlike the highly complicated plot of The Sign of Four, most of which happens abroad, this story is simple, easy to follow and perfectly set on the wild and atmospheric landscape of Dartmoor. In essence, the narrative is centred on an old family curse of a supernatural hound that killed dastardly villain Sir Hugo Baskerville. Rumours circulate around the village of Grimpen where the Baskerville family estate is situated that the hound has come back to stalk the family once more. Sir Charles Baskerville died mysteriously of fright and large animal footprints were found next to the body – 'Mr Holmes, they were the footprints of a gigantic hound!'

Before his heir, Sir Henry, takes up his inheritance and travels to the family home, he and family friend Doctor Mortimer consult Sherlock Holmes for advice. Holmes takes up the case, sending Watson to Dartmoor to accompany the baronet but insisting that he is too busy to go himself. He follows in secret, staying out on the moors and receiving reports from Watson as the situation develops - reports which he is actually rather complimentary about. In fact Watson receives various compliments from Holmes in this novel and their friendship seems deeper than ever. This includes the now famous line, 'It may be that you are not yourself luminous, but you are a conductor of light. Some people without genius have a remarkable power of stimulating it. I confess, my dear fellow, that I am very much in your debt.' Though Holmes does somewhat retract this later on – 'When I said that you stimulated me I meant, to be frank, that in noting your fallacies I was occasionally guided towards the truth.' Did he mean this, or was he just uncomfortable about having been so nice?

He does pay Watson another compliment when explaining to Sir Henry why he is sending Watson to accompany him back to Dartmoor – 'There is no man better worth having at your side when you are in a tight place. No one can say so more confidently than I.' This time he doesn't take it back.

Even Lestrade gets a compliment, albeit a bit half-hearted – 'Best of the professionals, I think.' So not completely convinced then? Lestrade returns the compliment upon his arrival at Dartmoor when he - 'Gazes at Holmes in a reverential way. He had learned a good deal from when they first worked together.'

We are treated to some brilliant deduction right from the start of the story, from the analysis of a walking stick to the mysterious warning letter Sir Henry receives while still in London. We are given pages of analysis over the letter which is simply brilliant and includes everything from Holmes identifying exactly which newspaper and article the words have been cut from to the fact they were cut with nail scissors.

Once the drama transfers to the moors the story starts to develop and we meet Stapleton, the strange man dancing around with his butterfly net and described as a naturalist – not to be confused with naturist (people who like to be naked) like I did when I first read the story! I pictured him bouncing around in the nude chasing butterflies like a hippy.

Stapleton is, of course, the villain of the piece (and fully clothed at all times). He is actually a Baskerville descendant and next in line to inherit the fortune if Sir Henry dies. He keeps a huge, ferocious, half-starved dog hidden in a mine shaft and gives it the hellish appearance by applying phosphorus to its muzzle creating bluish flames. The very site of it was enough to kill Sir Charles due to his weak heart. Stapleton finally sets the hound upon Sir Henry but Holmes, Watson and Lestrade are lying in wait to save the day.

We are treated to a happy, tidy ending with the dog shot dead, Sir Henry able to enjoy his inherited fortune and Stapleton suspected to have fallen into the Grimpen Mire and died. Hurrah!

The first thing that pops into my mind whenever I think of The Hound will always be that compelling image of Holmes upon the Black Tor – 'As far as I could judge, the figure was that of a tall, thin man. He stood with his legs a little separated, his arms folded, his head bowed, as if he were brooding over that enormous wilderness of peat and granite which lay before him. He might have been the very spirit of that terrible place.' I can really see him standing there in the moonlight, tails of his coat blowing in the wind as the mist and fog swirls around him. There is something about this story that really does stay with you and it's full of atmospheric strong images just like that one.

I love The Hound of the Baskervilles just as much as I did the first time I read it, if not more. I give it a confident 10 out of 10.

The Valley of Fear

Based on the real-life case of James McParland, a Pinkerton agent who testified against a secret society of Irish American coal-miners, this is another story with a complicated back-history. It's a tale of revenge, love, murder and Moriarty. Yes that old chestnut pops up again doing his 'arch-enemy' bit, still rather unconvincingly in my opinion.

The Valley is set before The Final Problem, which is strange considering Watson has never heard of Moriarty in that pivotal tale. As mistakes go, Sir Arthur made a pretty big one here but I forgive him, I always forgive him – the mysteriously changing wound, John and James Watson, it's all part of the fun really.

This story came out after the Final Problem, even though the adventure precedes it – confused? I know, just stick with me on this. This means that Final Problem is the first time we encounter Moriarty - he really does appear from nowhere. His inclusion in this story is just a re-education, a reminder of why he is Holmes' ultimate nemesis and frankly, a bit of an after-thought. If you've already read Final Problem and Empty House, you're done with Moriarty by the time you get to Valley of Fear. He's super-clever, evil and has a vast network of associates – yes we get it, got it last time thanks. In fact, didn't he disappear into a waterfall last time I read about him? Wish he had been left there to be honest. However, I must admit that I find Moriarty better developed here, a more sinister, less pantomime villain. I love the way Holmes explains to Inspector Macdonald how he knows the Professor's legitimate job is just a front. He explains that the professor only earns £700 a year from his legitimate job but owns a painting worth £4000 and pays Moran a yearly salary £6000.

The story begins in England with the supposed murder of John Douglas at Birlstone House in Sussex. But, as is often the way with Sherlock Holmes stories, the plot shifts abroad. This time it's to Vermissa Valley, a mining region in America. And it's another complicated one. John Douglas is actually alive, the victim is an intruder who had come to kill Douglas but got shot in the struggle. The wound destroyed his face so it was easy to pretend he was actually Douglas himself. The two men were both members of a secret society back in Vermissa Valley.

Using the alias of John McMurdo, Douglas (real name Birdy Edwards) infiltrated the secret society gaining their trust before trapping them and reporting their criminal activities to the police. He flees with his new wife, first to California then eventually to England after his wife dies of illness. Knowing he has been tracked down, Douglas tries to pass off the dead intruder as himself and ultimately flees to South Africa. Holmes subsequently learns that he has been lost overboard and suspects the hand of Moriarty.

A character with three names (John Douglas, John McMurdo and Birdy Edwards) is pretty darn confusing all by its self, but add in the rest of the plot, the broken-up time-line, the geographical shifts and, frankly, it's all a bit much for me. Perhaps I'm just a person of simple brain (gosh, Holmes would get so frustrated with me) but I did find myself losing the plot at times. It's not as bad as the confusing mess which makes up The Sign of Four but isn't far behind. I would rank the three long stories involving past misdemeanours on foreign shores in the following order regarding how well the plots hold together – A Study in Scarlet, The Valley of Fear then The Sign of Four. But, The Valley does have the best twist – the first time I read it, finding out that McMurdo was an undercover investigator was a big, satisfying surprise.

The story also includes some further insight into Holmes' character, particularly with regard to women. He is quite scathing about the female population with this sweeping generalisation - 'I am not a whole-souled admirer of womankind, as you are aware Watson...' But, later on, he does acknowledge the possibility of marrying one day and that he would want it to be a marriage of love -

'Should I ever marry, Watson, I should hope to inspire my wife with some feeling which would prevent her from being walked off by a housekeeper when my corpse was lying within a few yards of her.'

When the action shifts to Douglas' American past, Watson's narration becomes more poetic - telling a story rather than simply describing the action. Doyle is a great story-teller and paints an absorbing picture of the mining valley – 'Everywhere there were stern signs of the crudest battle of life, the rude work to be done, and the rude, strong workers who did it.' Reminding us yet again of the literary skill which often gets forgotten, overshadowed by his greatest creation – the character of Sherlock Holmes.

I have read this story at least four times now and seem to respond to it differently each time. On occasions I have found it absorbing, surprising and an enjoyable piece of escapism. Other times a bit confusing, over-complicated and lacking in further insight into Holmes and Watson's relationship. So I started re-reading it with more than a little scepticism. Husband declared that this was his least favourite long story but I did find myself defending it. There is much to enjoy, not least a good twist. However, the ending is disappointing and I would have preferred a much happier one. On balance, The Valley scores 7 out of 10.

The End of the Adventure... (Or is it?)

Well, that's it – 56 stories read and reviewed, four long stories read and reviewed, novel completed, second edition completed, blog still popular. Blimey, what an adventure. And it's all thanks to Sir Arthur Conan Doyle, sitting there in his surgery between patients and writing a character so intriguing that countless writers, actors, producers and artists have been inspired to re-imagine him ever since.

Re-reading his work and analysing it so carefully has reminded me of Conan Doyle's skill and talent – I feel humbled by what he achieved. The very least we can all do is try to protect his former home from destruction. So, you see, the adventure is actually far from over. There's Undershaw to protect and I have my dream of seeing Barefoot on Baker Street on the screen. But for a no-one from nowhere-land like me that's my greatest challenge, the process would probably fill a whole book by itself.

My husband would love to get his wife back after all these years of her head being buried in a book or the laptop, but I'm sure there are a few more novels left in me yet.

To all those who have read my blogs, bought my novel, bought this book and generally given me their support, I give you a massive "thank you". And to my husband Tim, the biggest thank you of all for putting up with me and my many projects.

Can't wait to find out what happens next as my adventures continue.

Also from Charlotte Anne Walters

Now in its 2nd edition, Barefoot on Baket Street is an epic novel which has received worldwide praise:

"I consider it to be one of the best pastiches I have read for a long time"

Sherlock Holmes Society of London Journal, Winter 2011

Undershaw Books

The publication date for 56 stories in 56 days was deliberately put in Sherlock Holmes Week to raise awareness for Save Undershaw – the campaign to save and restore Sir Arthur Conan Doyle's former home. Undershaw is where he brought Sherlock Holmes back to life, and should be preserved for future generations of Holmes fans.

Save Undershaw   www.saveundershaw.com

Sherlockology   www.sherlockology.com

MX Publishing   www.mxpublishing.com

You can read more about Sir Arthur Conan Doyle and Undershaw in Alistair Duncan's book (share of royalties to the Undershaw Preservation Trust) – An Entirely New Country and in the amazing compilation Sherlock's Home – The Empty House (all royalties to the Trust).

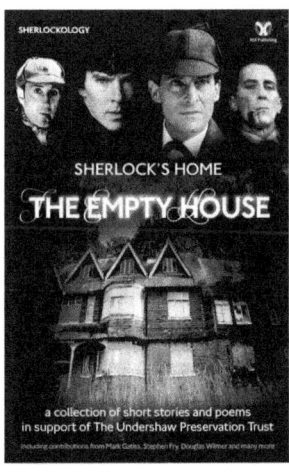 

Also From MX Publishing

Winners of the 2011 Howlett Literary Award (Sherlock Holmes book of the year) for '**The Norwood Author**' From one of the world's largest Sherlock Holmes publishers dozens of new novels from the top Holmes authors.
www.mxpublishing.com

Including our bestselling short story collections 'Lost Stories of Sherlock Holmes' and 'The Outstanding Mysteries of Sherlock Holmes'.

New in 2012 [Novels unless stated]:

Sherlock Holmes and the Plague of Dracula
Sherlock Holmes and The Adventure of The Jacobite Rose [Play]
Sherlock Holmes and The Whitechapel Vampire
Holmes Sweet Holmes
The Detective and The Woman: A Novel of Sherlock Holmes
Sherlock Holmes Tales From The Stranger's Room
The Sherlock Holmes Who's Who [Reference]
Sherlock Holmes and The Dead Boer at Scotney Castle
The Secret Journal of Dr Watson
A Professor Reflects on Sherlock Holmes [Essay Collection]
Sherlock Holmes of The Lyme Regis Legacy
Sherlock Holmes and The Discarded Cigarette [Short Novel]
Sherlock Holmes On The Air [Radio Plays]
Sherlock Holmes and The Murder at Lodore Falls
Untold Adventure of Sherlock Holmes
Sherlock Holmes and The Terrible Secret

  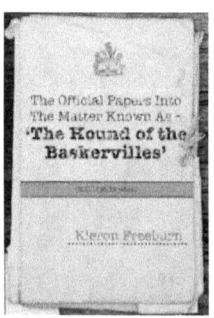

Also From MX Publishing

The Case of The Grave Accusation

The creator of Sherlock Holmes has been accused of murder. Only Holmes and Watson can stop the destruction of the Holmes legacy.

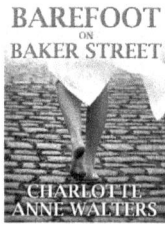

Barefoot on Baker Street (1st Ed)

Epic novel of the life of a Victorian workhouse orphan featuring Sherlock Holmes and Moriarty.

Case of Witchcraft

A tale of witchcraft in the Northern Isles, in which long-concealed secrets are revealed -- including some that concern the Great Detective himself!

www.mxpublishing.com

Also From MX Publishing

The Affair In Transylvania

Holmes and Watson tackle Dracula
in deepest Transylvania in this
stunning adaptation by film director
Gerry O'Hara

The London of Sherlock Holmes

400 locations including GPS co-
ordinates that enable Google Street
view of the locations around
London in all the Homes stories

I Will Find The Answer

Sequel to Rendezvous At The
Populaire, Holmes and Watson tackle
Dr.Jekyll.

www.mxpublishing.com

Also From MX Publishing

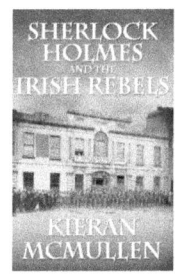

Sherlock Holmes and The Irish Rebels

It is early 1916 and the world is at war. Sherlock Holmes is well into his spy persona as Altamont.

The Punishment of Sherlock Holmes

"deliberately and successfully funny"

The Sherlock Holmes Society of London

No Police Like Holmes

It's a Sherlock Holmes symposium, and murder is involved. The first case for Sebastian McCabe.

www.mxpublishing.com

Also From MX Publishing

In The Night, In The Dark

Winner of the Dracula Society Award
– a collection of supernatural ghost
stories from the editor of the Sherlock
Holmes Society of London journal.

Sherlock Holmes and
The Lyme Regis Horror

Fully updated 2nd edition of this
bestselling Holmes story set in Dorset.

My Dear Watson

Winner of the Suntory Mystery Award
for fiction and translated from the
original Japanese. Holmes greatest
secret is revealed – Sherlock Holmes is
a woman.

www.mxpublishing.com

Also From MX Publishing

Sherlock Holmes Whos Who

All the characters from the entire canon catalogued and profiled.

Sherlock Holmes and The Lyme Regis Legacy

Sequel to the Lyme Regis Horror and Holmes and Watson are once again embroiled in murder in Dorset.

Sherlock Holmes and The Discarded Cigarette

London 1895. A well known author, a theoretical invention made real and the perfect crime.

www.mxpublishing.com